HAPPILY EVER AFTER

HAPPILY EVER AFTER

MELANIE MARTINS

Melanie Martins

BOOK ONE

BLOSSOM IN WINTER V

Melanie Martins, LLC
www.melaniemartins.com

First published in the United States by Melanie Martins, LLC in 2021.

ISBSN ebook 979-8-9852380-4-4

ISBN Paperback 979-8-9852380-0-6

Printed and bound by CPI Group (UK) Ltd, Croydon, CR0 4YY

DISCLAIMER

This novel is a work of fiction written in American-English and is intended for mature audiences. Names, characters, places, and incidents are either the product of the author's imagination or used fictitiously. Any resemblance to actual persons, living or dead, is entirely coincidental. This n ovel contains strong and explicit language, graphic sexuality, and other sensitive content that may be disturbing for some readers.

To all of you, my dear readers.
Thank you.

READING ORDER

Blossom in Winter series (Petra & Alex's story)

1. Blossom in Winter
2. Lured into Love
3. Lured into Lies
4. Defying Eternity
5. Happily Ever After: Part 1 (You are here), 2, 3, and 4

Van den Bosch series

1. Roxanne.
2. Andries.
3. Elise.
4. Dan.
5. Julia.
6. Sebastian.
7. Hannah
8. Johan

CHAPTER 1

Manhattan, November 18, 2021
Petra

"I'll be back in a few hours!" I call cheerily, letting the door click shut behind me.

As soon as I'm alone, the cheery facade falls away and I'm fighting the urge to look back. Logically, I know the babies are safe and sound with Lily, but I can't help worrying. Leaving them behind still tugs at my heartstrings, no matter how much I do to reassure myself of their comfort.

Maybe it's because of all those weeks in the NICU, or maybe it's because after having such a high-risk pregnancy, I'm still struggling to come to terms with the fact that everything is actually going okay for once.

In fact, when we had finally been able to bring Jasmine and Jasper home, I kept wondering when the other shoe would drop. Surely, something was bound to go wrong. Things were never this easy... right?

Wrong. Besides the normal stresses that came along with being a new parent, everything has gone much better than expected. The twins continue to grow in slow, steady increments with no major health scares, and Alex and I have been working hard to repair our marriage completely. There may be all the love in the world between us, but our marriage had been a trial by fire from the start. If we wanted to stay strong, we had to work diligently to fill in any of the missing gaps.

The plan today is to ease one of my other anxieties: the fear of leaving the babies. During their hospital stay, I had watched their every waking moment every single day—often falling asleep with my head on the glass incubator—so realizing that I could leave them and live my own life from time to time is still a hard pill I'm trying to swallow. There's always that fear lingering inside me that I'll receive a phone call from Lily letting me know that something terrible happened to them.

Regardless, I'm thankful every day that Alex was able to secure Lily as our live-in nurse. Whenever I start to spiral, she is there, guiding me through motherhood with a gentle but steady hand. But Lily is a realist, and she is adamant that until I regain my own life, hobbies, and happiness outside of my role as a mother, there will always be a well of unhappiness inside of me. So, with her encouragement, I have accepted a lunch date with Emma today.

It's nothing too crazy, but at least I'm out of the condo for a few hours, which is a step in the right direction… but funnily enough, my feet refuse to pull me farther along. I want to stay home, but at the same time, I'm dying to get out of here for just a little while.

You're being ridiculous, I tell myself, and step by difficult step, I make my way to the idling car where my driver, Zach, is waiting.

Emma is leaning against the sedan, her mittened hands crammed into the pockets of her leather coat as she finishes off a cigarette. She perks up as soon as she sees me, dropping the cigarette on the pavement and crushing it with the toes of her boot before hustling over to me.

Emma is on the front line of high-end fashion, always dressed impeccably in the darkest of colors. With our opposing sense of style, we make an odd-looking pair, but neither of us could care any less.

"I have to admit, I was starting to doubt if you were still coming," Emma says, raising one perfectly arched brow.

"Honestly, I did hesitate a few times." I look down at the ground. "Am I getting on your nerves, with all of this refusing-to-leave-the-babies nonsense?"

Emma snorts. "Babe, there have been numerous times in our relationship you have grated on my nerves, but this definitely isn't one of them."

I blow out a relieved breath, and Emma smiles, her white teeth brilliant against her carmine lipstick.

She holds open the car door for me, continuing, "Don't worry, I'll let you know if you're annoying me."

I roll my eyes as she gets into the back seat with me. Emma didn't really have room to talk about being annoying. The number of times she'd invited me to hang out only for me to realize it was to go to a club or underground party for her to get wasted because of some shitty argument she had had with Yara are more than I can count on one hand; not to mention the numerous calls I had gotten from local police stations to come and pick her up. In my opinion, Emma is getting too attached to her, and sooner or later, this affair is going to end.

And it won't be in a good way.

But I promised her I won't give my two cents on the matter anymore and I've kept that promise. At least for now...

* * *

"I can't eat another bite." Emma groans, pushing her plate away, and I laugh as she leans back in the wrought-iron chair, holding her belly dramatically.

Pushing around the last of my stuffed mushrooms on my plate, I soak in the domestic warmth of the moment. My best friend and I, enjoying lunch at a quaint little cafe, our table tucked into the corner while the hum and chatter of the other guests flow over us. It's exactly how life should be.

Emma had called this morning and asked if I could pull away from the twins for a few hours today so we could have some honest-to-God girl time. I'd been trying to get away in little snippets of moments here and there, slowly building up to leave my babies with Lily for an afternoon in preparation for our outing. There is no one I'd trust with my kids more in the world than Lily, and yet, I feel the distance and guilt pulling on me every time I leave.

Fortunately, after the uncomfortableness of leaving my sleeping infants behind had faded away, I finally managed to relax in Emma's company. And after a while, it began to feel just like old times.

She had invited me out to a small lunch cafe downtown, decorated with a New Orleans theme. We'd shared some mushroom tapas, an avocado pizza, and chatted, sipping our coffees while we now waited for the bill.

"Is your dad still mad at you?" she asks, seemingly out of the blue.

The question catches me off guard, but I knew sooner or later she would want to get an update on the situation. "He's still a bit grumpy, yeah," I confess. "Columbia is really important to him, and taking the semester off was a big blow in his eyes." When my dad learned I wasn't attending classes this semester, he became furious with me. It's not like I wouldn't be resuming classes again in January, but he was totally against my decision for wanting to take some time off from college. Despite my dad not talking to me for the past few days, I don't regret my decision—it's not every day that you're a first-time mom, and after everything I went through for the twins, I need some time to heal and to settle into this new life.

"Damn, so ridiculous," she comments. "Are you still gonna return to classes in January?"

"Yes," I answer. "I promised him I'd graduate, and that's what I intend to do."

A quick silence settles afterward as I realize there isn't much more to catch up on; Emma can't stay away from the twins, and every few days security phones to let us know that

Emma is on her way into the condo. She doesn't even ask anymore, and honestly, it's nice to hand a baby off to her and the other to Lily or Alex so I can go take a nice, quiet nap. After everything that happened these past months, life has been so...normal. And, for the very first time in so long, comfortable. I had spent so many months neck-deep in chaos that these quiet days still catch me off guard.

There is no tenseness between Emma and me anymore. Her relationship with Yara has been pushed far into the back of my mind, and despite knowing they have their issues, I refrain from interfering. As I come to think of it, if I had ever had any doubt about our friendship pulling through, it had all vanished when I saw her face the first time she saw Jasmine and Jasper.

Emma and I... We are strong on our own, but even stronger together.

A small smile plays over my face, and I guess I've drifted off because Emma taps my foot with hers under the table.

"Hello? Earth to Petra, are you done?" Emma jokes.

I turn my smile to her, lying my napkin beside my plate and exhaling. "I'm ready whenever you are."

Emma tosses back the last of her latte and we pay, throwing on our coats and heading out into the November cold. It hasn't reached the depths of winter yet, so the cold is still relatively bearable, but coming off of a warm October, it's still highly unpleasant.

Emma shivers and zips her leather jacket closed, tucking a heavy gray scarf into the neck. I'd chosen a white, knee-length puffer and my favorite suede gloves. Manhattan has its upsides, but the weather isn't one of them.

"Should we call the driver?" Emma asks, pulling her hair out from where it has gotten tangled in her scarf.

I pull out my phone to call Zach but pause. I'm not ready to go home yet. I crane my neck, looking down the road to get my bearings about where we are when the area finally clicks with me.

"Not yet, actually. Do you want to walk down to an art gallery with me? We are close to The Artemis Room, one of my favorites. I haven't been there in so long!" I exclaim. Emma purses her mouth, glances at her watch and considers the offer before nodding.

"Alright, I've got some more time. Lead the way."

We walk quietly together for a while, our hands shoved in our pockets for warmth.

I like this quietness—it's the easy, silent companionship of old friends. But eventually, Emma speaks up.

"Still settling into mom life well?" she asks, her mouth quirking at the corners.

I scoff. "Like you even have to ask. You practically live at my condo now. I think you're actually Jasmine's best friend rather than mine at this point."

Her grin is full now. "Yeah, well, I know all about the twins, especially my new bestie Jasmine, but you and I never have time to talk without Lily, Maria, or Alex hovering around like watchful hawks. So now that we're alone, tell me how you're *really* feeling."

I ponder her question thoughtfully. There have been moments that every first-time parent goes through, except my trials are doubled—because, well, twins. Once the babies had come home, we had many sleepless nights. Sometimes, because of the anxiety of letting them out of our sight for even a minute, and other times because they decided three a.m. was the best time to scream their heads off. But all in all, we had settled into a routine with Lily's help, and I had slowly regained my time.

Alex had been volcanic in his enthusiasm for the twins, at first, dragging our room designer, Leonardo, out to the nursery multiple times a week to blather on about soothing colors and Feng Shui. I'd also find him lingering over the bassinets all night long, running his long fingers down the babies' soft cheeks as they slept, a look of awe on his face every time. He has only just begun to allow himself a full eight hours of sleep.

Funnily enough, after months of begging him to sleep in bed with me, I was all but forcing him into the bedroom to get some sleep without having to wake up with the babies throughout the night. Despite him being on paternity leave, Alex still had to answer emails, phone calls, and attend some business meet-ups, and it wasn't doing either of us any good for him to be like a zombie in the mornings. Thankfully, the twins are getting older, and the midnight crying jags are finally slowing down.

I turn to Emma as we walk and shrug. "I'm pretty tired, and constantly worried about them, but I read in my postnatal books that all of those emotions are normal for new moms. So, maybe I just need to learn how to relax some more, but overall I'm doing okay."

"And, um, what about that depression you had?" she asks, her voice laced with worry. "Is it solved once and for all?"

"Oh," I utter, now understanding exactly what she meant when she asked how I was *really* doing. "Yeah, it's over now."

And thank God it is. The surge of adrenaline-fueled joy after my successful delivery of two high-risk twins had faded about a week postpartum, and in its place, I'd been alarmed to find a vast emptiness. The long hours in the NICU, listening to the incessant beeping of the machines had made time slow to a miserable crawl. Every day the babies got stronger, and it should've been cause for celebration, but for some reason, even that miracle felt hollow like it was happening to someone else. I went through the motions as anybody would; pumping breast milk, skin to skin contact when the twins were well enough, learning how to care for a preemie with a feeding tube... but it was all just something I had to do. Inside, I was exhausted.

I still recall when Marianna had crouched in front of the exam table when I told her how I was feeling, two weeks after the delivery. She took my hands in hers, patting them gently. *"Postpartum depression is extremely common, Petra. You don't have to be embarrassed to talk about it with me, okay?"*

She had explained that a normal pregnancy caused a woman's body to be so full of hormones and endorphins that when they have all been flushed away after birth, even the healthiest mothers could feel this distant sadness looming over them. I had all of those hormones, too, but coupled with the emotional stress of the high-risk pregnancy and Alex's trial, I was a prime candidate for full-blown postpartum depression.

Thank goodness I had been upfront with Marianna. We did a short-term course of medication paired with weekly therapy appointments with a therapist specially trained for postpartum cases. Apparently, pregnancies as traumatic as mine could have long-lasting mental effects if not treated swiftly and properly, and I'm thankful every day that I was able to get mine handled as soon as possible.

Emma nods. "Alright, I trust you, babe. But if you ever get overwhelmed and need me to spirit you away, let me know."

I'm touched. We'd all been so worried about Jasmine and Jasper that having them home and thriving was like a dream come true. I actually had to adjust and leave some of my worries behind. I'm not high-risk Petra anymore, I'm mom Petra. Except, I've never been mom Petra before, and I'm still finding the proper footing.

"Thanks for asking. Sometimes I even forget about myself in all the chaos." I chuckle at her concerned glance. "Really, Emma. I'm great. I've got the best support system of all time between Alex, Lily, Maria, you, and Matt. I mean, what could go wrong?"

She snorts. "Oh, yeah, Matt. That's a whole different conversation… but hey, what gallery are we going to again?"

"It's called The Artemis Room. It's this great family-run gallery that features local artists. I had always dreamed about being featured there when I was younger. I haven't been in a while."

The entrance of the gallery comes into view, the burnished silver sign catching the midday sun as it filters through the buildings. The name of the gallery floats above a crescent moon framed by antlers, making a simple but striking logo that is easy to remember. I have always loved it.

Besides the sign, though… the gallery has seen better days. The once pale gray stone has darkened with age and neglect, and moss has gathered in the corners and flourishes of the building. Worst of all, the gallery's two famous gargoyles, perched on the corners of the roof, look rather dreadful. They are just as dark and decrepit as the rest of the building, but leaf litter clings to their fierce heads and roaring mouths. To add insult to injury, a bird had built a nest between the teeth of the left gargoyle.

The whole thing makes me grimace and wrinkle my nose, but I shake it off. It's still The Artemis Room, no matter what. If I didn't look too closely, it didn't look *that* much different from the last time I'd seen it.

It's all here, everything from my memory, except for one thing…

The moving trucks are out front, being filled with artwork and furniture by grumpy-faced moving men. When I realize what's going on, my heart drops to my feet.

"Hey!" I yell, running up to the moving man with the clipboard standing at the front of the truck. "What's going on here?"

The man waves me away, pointing to the gallery. "Old tenant's in there. Go ask her. I don't know shit."

I recoil at his foul mouth before stomping back to Emma, incensed. "Come on, we're going in."

Emma looks skeptical. "Petra, it's clearly closed…"

I ignore her, brushing past her to enter the building. I hear her sigh, resigned, and follow behind me. Everything looks like I remember: the gauzy curtains on the windows protecting the paintings from direct sunlight, the antique chandeliers dripping with crystals, and the two stone statues of the gallery's eponymous goddess, Artemis, flanking the entryway, a bow clutched in her granite hands.

But besides the nostalgia, The Artemis Room is in a sad state, the once decorated walls empty and the lights turned up high, casting the emptiness of the place in stark relief. It hurts my soul to see it this way when it had been so full of life the last time I visited.

I find the tenant, who has always gone by Ms. Artemis herself, in the very back, tapping her kohl-lined eyes with a lacy handkerchief. She sniffs when she sees me, adjusting her emerald-green bohemian dress. She looks so much older than when I had seen her last. Her long raven hair is now shot through with white.

"Ms. Artemis," I exclaim. She doesn't recognize me, though I didn't expect her to, among the thousands of patrons she has had over the years. "What's going on? Why are they taking everything away?"

"Oh, dear girl, I have finally decided to move to Florida, and I just can't afford to pay for someone to run the gallery in my stead. It's just too big. So I'm moving on." Her dark brown eyes are still swimming with tears. "I just didn't expect it to be so painful."

"You've run this place for as long as I can remember," I tell her somberly, turning in a slow circle to take it all in.

Ms. Artemis nods, tapping her eyes again. "Yes, yes... But all good things must end."

Emma finally catches up with me, and she plants her hands on her hips as she looks around. "This is a great space.

Buyers are going to be champing at the bit to bid on it," she remarks.

The mention of buyers sparks something in my mind. I take a step back and observe the space again, but this time not from the view of a sentimental past guest, but a potential buyer. Emma is right, the space is amazing for downtown Manhattan, and I know that the upper floor is a recently renovated office space.

It all starts to take shape in my mind, the gallery full of art again, but this time, art of my choosing. And upstairs, the staff for the Gatt-Dieren Art Fund. I'd been running the whole thing virtually for so long that the idea of having a real office space for my fund to expand is amazing. Before I had found out I was pregnant, I had laid out the financial plan to show it to Mike, raise some capital, and develop the fund even more, but with everything else going on, it had fallen to the wayside.

What better way to find myself again than to start the business I had always dreamed of?

"Ms. Artemis, is the owner of the building willing to rent, or even sell? Can I get his contact information?" I say, reining in the excitement in my voice.

The older woman sighs, pulling a business card out from her vintage clutch and hands it to me. "Here you go, dear. But I'll forewarn you, he's desperate to get rid of the place. I've been renting it out for over thirty years, and the idea of starting fresh with a new tenant has old Nico up in arms. He told me he's selling it to a buyer that wants to gut the place and turn it into a restaurant or something."

The card simply reads "NICO TUCCI" with a phone number inscribed underneath. I slide it into my coat pocket as I hear Emma groan at Ms. Artemis's words.

"Of course, someone would be so overtly willing to tear down all this historic architecture. What a waste," Emma complains, dragging the toe of her shoe over the antique tile as she speaks.

"Not so fast," I reassure her. "I'm going to buy it!"

Both women raise their eyebrows and look at each other. "This is a bit of a split-second decision," Emma comments apprehensively. I shake my head.

"It's fate! Just think about it. My own gallery, and one day it will belong to the twins. By then, the Gatt-Dieren Art Fund should be a hugely successful dynasty for them to take over. It has to be fate. Why else would I have even thought of this place after so long?"

Emma seems to think about it but looks unconvinced. "Shouldn't you talk to Alex about this first?"

I shake my head. "No. This is my fund. He'd want me to pursue it myself. He's always telling me to branch out, anyway."

I take a long look around the space again, awash in memories of all the fond times I had here and giddy with the idea of my art, and the art of other artists I love, hanging here in the near future. I look back to Ms. Artemis, who is tapping the corner of her eyes with a tissue, and hold my hand out to her. I would hug her if it wasn't mildly inappropriate, so we shake hands and I bid her goodbye, taking her number down so I can tell her any news relating to the building.

Emma and I head back outside, and I ask her to call my driver while I call the owner of the building. Emma agrees and takes a few steps away from me to make the call and I type the number into my phone, feeling full of adrenaline.

"This is Nico. How can I help you?" an accented voice comes from the other end of the line, and I clear my throat, amping myself up for the negotiation.

"Hello, my name is Petra Van Gatt. I'm calling regarding what was formerly known as The Artemis Room. I'm interested in purchasing the building."

Nico grunts. "Too late, I'm afraid. I've already agreed to sell it to a big hospitality brand for a new restaurant, or bar, or something along those lines. Sorry about that, have a nice —"

"Wait!" I butt in. "This was a meaningful location for me when I was younger, and I'm willing to pay beyond what they are offering. I'd love to sit down and go over numbers with you."

I listen hopefully, but Nico just grunts again. "In my younger days, I would jump on an offer like that, but the truth is the paperwork is almost done and they already paid a deposit for the place. I'm sticking with them."

"Mr. Tucci, no disrespect meant, but this is a building in downtown Manhattan. There is *always* someone that will pay more. Why settle on the first offer? You can always give back the deposit."

Nico sighs loudly. "I already told you, miss. I'm tired. I don't want to do negotiations, and I surely don't want to sit down and talk to you and your husband about it," he argues back.

I'm silent for a moment, getting angrier by the second. I had been so sure I would be able to handle this on my own, but of course, Nico would recognize I'm Alex's wife, given the amount of news coverage we had gotten during the court cases. Everyone in town did. But it pisses me off that he's assuming this is something my husband is involved in. "Again, Mr. Tucci, no disrespect, but I never mentioned my husband, so why would you bring him up? Do you have an issue with him?"

Nico scoffs. "No, Ms. Van Gatt, it's because I already gave my word to that company. The deal is nearly done. Plus, do you know they're paying cash? Cash! In a market like this!" He laughs, and I can almost see him shaking his head on the other end of the phone. "For someone my age, convenience is worth quite a bit more than quantity."

I fight to not grind my teeth at his smug tone. "Alright, Nico. Then allow me to counter. I'll pay cash, and I'll have my people do all the paperwork and get all the permits updated. All you'll have to do is sign the paper and kick back and relax. What do you say? Let me know your schedule and I'll get us penciled in for a sit-down."

"Well, well. I'm still not convinced that you are worth the trouble, Ms. Van Gatt, or should I say Petra, since apparently we're on a first-name basis now? Regardless, it's an excellent offer." Nico pauses, a quick silence ensuing. "I'll tell you what. I'll consider it. Keep your phone on you, eh?" If I'm not mistaken, I believe I hear a trace of respect in Nico's voice.

"I will, Mr. Tucci, but my patience isn't endless. Talk to you soon."

He barks another laugh. "Goodbye, Ms. Van Gatt."

I push my phone back into my purse, not even feeling the bite in the air because of how hot with anger I am. I may be young, but I've grown up around these know-it-all proprietors. I can hold my own and being talked down to is one of my biggest annoyances.

Emma finds her way back to me, an amused look on her face. "Oh, you look pissed."

"Sorry, I hate arrogant dudes," I seethe.

She looks at me, a smirk rising across her face. "Really?"

And I know exactly what she means by that. "Oh, Emma, stop it!" I slap her arm playfully. "Alex is different."

Yet, she breaks in laughter. "I'm sure he is…"

It's such an open and relaxed moment among friends. I'm so glad we've gotten back to this point and are completely comfortable with each other again. I'm not sure I could have gone my whole life feeling weird around Emma.

Zach pulls up and we shuffle into the car, wanting to escape the brisk chill in the air. Since Emma had left her vehicle back at the condo, we ride back together, shucking our coats in the car's warmth and relaxing in the leather seats. After a quiet few minutes, Emma speaks up.

"You know, Alex would probably have a brand-new gallery built for you from the ground up, exactly how you wanted it. Why bother with this old building?"

I ponder her question for a moment. "There's something to be said for history, and yeah, maybe a touch of nostalgia. But that building means something to me, and it has good bones. It's full of personality, memories, and it—"

Emma holds up a hand to stop me. "Alright, alright, I get it. I just didn't want this to be a spur-of-the-moment decision that you make out of nowhere. It'd look wonderful for your gallery to be focused out of a historic building. It kind of shows that you value art in all its forms, on canvas and architecturally, right?"

I like that thought. Maybe people would take the Art Fund even more seriously if we based it out of somewhere like the old Artemis Room, and not some prefab office building. Now that I'm fully convinced, I'm even more nervous at the idea of Nico not calling me back. I may have sounded confident on the phone, but really, this was something that I really wanted. It would be a lot more painful to have it snatched away now.

We talk about other random subjects on the drive back to the condo, but in the back of my mind, I'm still thinking about The Artemis Room, considering how to decorate it, where all the offices would go, and even what our opening night would look like. I lose track of time and before I know it, we're home and I'm waving goodbye to Emma, heading back inside.

Reaching the entryway, I shimmy out of my coat and hand it to Maria, who greets me at the door. My head is still swimming with gallery ideas until Lily comes around the corner, dressed in a sunflower yellow wrap dress while holding a very awake Jasper, who has one of her dozens and dozens of braids clutched in his chubby fist. Lily's expression is weary but cheerful.

"They've decided to trade attitudes today. Jasmine is having a nice nap, but her brother here has decided he's never sleeping again." She looks down at the baby in her arms. "Would you like to see your mommy now, little prince?"

"I don't care if he does or not," I answer jokingly, already rushing towards her, my smile spreading up to my ears. "Give him here." I reach out for my son and Lily hands him over.

He relinquishes the braid after I pry it from his chubby fist, and Lily immediately gathers her braids into an enormous bun on the top of her head, securing it with a band she had been wearing on her wrist. "Really, it's my fault. I should've known better than to have my hair down around these little grabbers." Lily kisses Jasper's tiny fist before releasing him to me fully.

Jasper is usually the quieter of my two angels, often watching us with wide, interested eyes while his sister screams the walls down. I breathe in his wonderful baby smell, kissing his soft, round cheek as he huffs, trying to grab at my earrings. I laugh, holding him even closer.

Lily runs her hands down her dress, smoothing it out before continuing. "He's been fed, and I tried to put him down for a nap with Jasmine, but he was extremely uninterested, as you can tell."

"He's not interested in much except for eating these days," I joke, tapping his little nose with the tip of my finger.

"Well, he is a male, so he may never grow out of that phase," Lily quips, watching as Jasper tries to shove his fist in his mouth. "I'm going to go take my break and run a few errands since you're home. There are some bottles in the refrigerator. Just have Maria pop them in the bottle warmer if our little prince gets hungry again soon."

"I don't know what I would do without you, Lily," I tell her as she shrugs on her coat and grabs her bag.

"Ah, Petra. You've blossomed into such a wonderful mother. It's my pleasure to be here and watch the little warriors grow so strong, and to help you along the way."

I'm touched, and I give her a one-armed hug before she departs. "Thank you, Lily. Enjoy your break."

CHAPTER 2

Petra

I take Jasper up to my bed and try to read to him a bit while he tries fighting sleep as hard as he can. Eventually, my little man dozes off into a fitful nap and I take a quick snooze with him. But about twenty minutes later, Jasmine lets us know, with no room for negotiation, that it's time to get up. I groan, scooping sleepy Jasper up and depositing him in his bassinet while I retrieve Jasmine. Jasper's eyes flutter a few times before he resumes his nap, and I take his much more awake sister out into the living area with me.

During my pregnancy, I had made a concentrated effort to dress attractively and look put together, even when I was just spending the day indoors. It brought me joy to see the look of heat and appreciation in Alex's eyes when he would see me. But I fell into my old habits of comfy outfits just quickly after their birth. So now, instead of designer dresses and beautifully tailored clothes, I find myself spending a good portion of my time in various pairs of Lululemon leggings and tops, my hair braided or pulled into a ballerina bun on top of my head. One needed to be comfortable and dressed in athletic clothing in order to keep up with the needs of two infants.

I braid my hair in the bathroom mirror, having handed off Jasmine to Maria for a moment, and think of Lily and her gorgeous wardrobe, full of bright color, and how she always looks so put together, even after a whole day with the twins. I guess if you deal with babies for a living, you eventually figure out how to be fashionable again.

My new venture into the best of athleisure wear wasn't without its perks, though. I recall the day I was standing on my tiptoes in the kitchen, reaching for my favorite tea mug on the top shelf, when I heard Alex enter the kitchen behind me and suck in a breath. I was suddenly aware of how my shirt had been riding up, displaying inches of my back and the skin-tight fit of my leggings. I had prepared to whip around and tell him he wasn't allowed to make fun of my casual wear, but I didn't have time.

Alex had come up behind me, his hands skimming up my hips to rest on my ass before growling in my ear, "*These ridiculous pants are going to be the death of me, you know that? Seeing you prance around all day, just this single layer between me and your skin.*"

He had nipped at my ear, making me giggle, and I had led him to the bedroom, intent on showing him how incredible his praise made me feel. Tea was all but forgotten that day.

Even now I blush thinking about all the clandestine hookups we have had in the kitchens and corners, having so little time between babies, pediatrician appointments, and Alex's work schedule. It rarely ever progressed to full-blown sex, but we had begun to come back together as a married couple, and it was everything I had been craving for the past months. I love Alex, and I love seeing how much Alex loves me. I can only hope that we continue to grow in our passion for one another.

It brings a smile to my face as I touch up the light makeup I had worn for lunch and leave the bathroom to retrieve Jasmine from Maria.

"Thanks, Maria. I just had to clean up a little for dinner," I tell her, hefting the baby into my arms.

"Not a problem, ma'am. Mr. Van Dieren called and said he would be home shortly."

"Great!" I can't help but smile. I love it when Alex is able to make it home to have dinner with me.

I head with Jasmine, who is squirming in my arms like an eel, into the living area, spreading out her tummy time mat and laying her down gently, keeping an eye on her wobbly head. She screeches, not a fan of tummy time, but I pat her diapered behind and take a seat on the floor next to her.

"Come on, princess. You know the deal. Tummy time first, and then you can have some milk," I tell her. She looks unconvinced, grunting a few times before making an earnest effort at turning over.

We had expected Jasmine to progress slower than Jasper, all of her health concerns considered, but so far she has been keeping pace with her brother—except for this one thing.

Jasper could roll in both directions and had moved on to trying to raise himself up on all fours, but Jasmine had been struggling with the rolling part.

Alex hadn't seemed worried. I even chuckle as I remember him saying, *"Jasper's got all that extra weight to give him momentum, not to mention his, uh…"* We had been sitting on the floor with the babies and Alex had covered Jasper's ears with his hands before whispering covertly to Jasmine and me, *"His enormous head."*

"Knock it off! His head is perfect, and Jasmine will catch up, won't you, princess? She just needs a little more time," I had told him, pretending to be scandalized on my son's behalf.

Back in the present moment, Jasmine finally manages to make it onto her side before letting out another frustrated screech. Her tiny face flushes with effort, so I place her back on her stomach. "You've got it, Jas. You're a strong survivor, remember?"

She huffs adorably at me, babbling. Right then, Lily returns from her break, and Jasmine's frustrated noises switch to excitement as her face lights up, chunky legs kicking hard when Lily makes her way over to us, sitting gracefully on the floor beside me.

"She's holding her head up incredibly well in this position. We'll count it as a win," Lily says, smiling warmly. "The rolling will come, Petra. Don't worry. All babies are different."

I blow out a breath. "I know. It's just… she and Jasper are sort of the same, right? They're twins, after all."

"Well, yes, but look at it like a race. Jasper had a significant head start, and Jasmine is catching up in her own time. At the end of the race, they will have both crossed the finish line, right? So no worries."

"I guess you're right." I run my hand gently over the sparse, soft brown hair on Jasmine's head.

Lily and I work with Jasmine for a while longer, eventually getting a nearly complete rollover from her. She jumps when we cheer for her, her pale blue eyes wide, and we both laugh.

After another thirty minutes, Alex returns home, his suit coat already off and slung over his shoulder. "Hello, ladies."

Like earlier at the cafe with Emma, Alex coming in and bending down to give me a quick kiss before heading to our room to change out of his work clothes is so sweetly domestic that I can't help but grin.

"Go on and join your husband," Lily tells me, shooing me away. "I'll take care of the babies. Enjoy your dinner."

"But," I start to protest, but she shakes her head.

"It's literally what you pay me for. Now go on."

"Fine. You can feed the little missy now as I think she's hungry, and Jasper when he gets up." I give Jasmine a quick peck on the head and make my way to the dining room to meet Alex.

I pause, slipping into the bathroom for a moment to check my phone, hoping to see a text or missed call from Nico Tucci. The screen is just as blank as it has been all afternoon and evening. I didn't want to be naïve, but I had really thought that my offer of taking care of every little detail of the sale would have piqued his interest enough so that he would at least give me the time of day.

I sigh, blowing a loose piece of hair out of my face while shoving my phone back into my pocket. I think back on Emma telling me that Alex would build me a gallery from the ground up if I wanted, and I also knew that if I asked, Alex would go to bat for me against Tucci; maybe using some of his contacts would give me a better chance of winning the ability to buy the building. But that fund is mine, and I want to be the one to make it flourish with my own two hands. Not by relying on someone else's help.

I'll have to put the thought out of my mind for dinner. Alex could for sure read the stress on my face and in my body language, and if I tell him everything, it could go one of two ways. He would either pull his cell out and start making calls to secure the place for me, or he'd wave the idea of purchasing such an old building off and insist we start making plans on a building plan for a new gallery and office space.

The latter was more likely. Alex appreciates vintage architecture, but that appreciation didn't bleed over into his business. He'd insist on everything being state of the art, streamlined, and efficient. Any other time I'd agree with him, function over nostalgia, but... I wanted the building where the soul of The Artemis Room lives. I want it more than I had wanted anything in a long while.

I take a few deep breaths, forcing the thoughts away, ready to just have a peaceful dinner with my husband. It has only been a few hours, really. Tucci could call any time. There isn't any reason to freak out just yet.

Still, though. I'm worried that he already signed the new landlords.

Changed into his casual clothing, Alex is reclining in his dining room chair, scrolling through his phone when I walk in. He sets the device down as I take my seat, settling in. There is already a huge kale salad waiting for us, as well as a frosted glass of cucumber water for me.

"How was work?" I ask, loading my plate with kale.

He shrugs. "It was alright. We are starting to expand our biotech portfolio and fundraise for next year, so all good," he says, looking at me as I eat. "Didn't you tell me you were going out for lunch with Emma today? How did that go?"

"It was nice to get out alone, but it was also nice to come home afterward. Makes me realize everything isn't going to fall apart if I let myself leave the babies sometimes," I tell him, but when I think of the lunch my mind immediately goes back to the gallery, and the thought leaves a pit in my stomach.

I guess something flashes across my face because Alex sets his fork down with a frown. "Something wrong?"

I shake my head. "Nothing, just thinking of some things I need to do tomorrow," I tell him, composing a forced smile.

Alex looks unconvinced, leaning forward with his elbow on the table and resting his chin in his hands. "Out with it, Petra."

I groan, rubbing my face with my hands. "It's silly…"

"It's not silly if it has you this worried, love. Let's hear it," Alex coerces, his voice soft and coaxing.

Fine. He's got me. "It's really not a big deal, but after lunch, Emma and I took a short walk to check out this gallery I've always loved called The Artemis Room."

Alex nods while I speak. "I've heard of it. I think it got featured a few times on the news. Anyway, continue."

"Probably. It used to be much more popular. But anyway, we walked down to the gallery and there were moving trucks outside! We went inside and the old renter was there. She said she's moving out and heading to Florida and that she had broken off her lease." I take a deep breath, preparing to launch into my explanation of my business idea. "I've always really loved the place, and it's in this beautiful old stone building with a grand staircase and offices on the second floor. I asked Ms. Artemis, the original renter, for the building owner's information and I called him. About purchasing the building."

Alex raises his eyebrows, leaning back in his chair. "Really? As a gallery?"

I twist the tablecloth between my fingers nervously as I continue, trying my best to sound confident. "Sort of. A gallery downstairs, but it would be linked to the Gatt-Dieren Art Fund that I would run out of the second floor. Some of the artists that I invested in would be featured in the gallery downstairs, and we could hold events to showcase the lesser-known artists in the city."

"It's not a *terrible* idea," Alex muses. "Is the upstairs an actual functioning space? It hasn't fallen into disrepair or anything of the sort?"

"No, Ms. Artemis used to feature her own artwork and hold private events upstairs. She always kept the place immaculate. No one wants to go to a dusty gallery," I assure him.

"Then it sounds like a sound business venture. What has you second-guessing yourself here?" Alex asks curiously.

I exhale. This was part of the story I didn't want to get into. "Like I said, I called the owner, and he told me he's already in the final steps of selling the building...to a hospitality brand to turn it into a restaurant." I pinch the bridge of my nose between my fingers, already feeling the annoyance rising in me again. "They're going to gut the place and ruin any of the appeal of the original building. The whole gallery will be ruined."

"Especially if they serve food. You can never get the smell of fryer grease out of a building," Alex agrees, his tone thoughtful. "You negotiated, I assume?"

"Yes. Probably too eagerly though," I confess. "But that was this afternoon, and he hasn't gotten back to me. I know that isn't any time, really, but since he said he was so close to signing the paperwork with them..." I poke at the salad on my plate. "I don't know, I get the feeling it's a lost cause."

Alex reaches across the table and takes my hands in his. "Not everything goes through easily. It's one of the more unpleasant parts of business. But you'll get used to this side of things, love."

"I know... I just wish my first, big disappointment wasn't something so meaningful to me."

Alex stands and comes over to my side of the table, tilting my head up with a finger beneath my chin and kissing me soundly on the mouth. "Just give it time to breathe, wife. Everything will work out in the end."

I grin as he walks back to his seat, and before he sits down again, I covertly check my phone one more time. Nothing, of course. Without a second thought, I lock the screen and place the phone back in my pocket. Alex is right. Worrying about the gallery constantly would not help Tucci decide any faster.

Instead, I focus on dinner with Alex. Sometimes I just like to watch him speak. I just love how he gestures with his hands and how animated his face is when he's telling me about something that he's interested in.

Dinner ends around seven pm, and we bid Lily goodnight. She heads to her room in the finished basement of the condo that we've outfitted to function as its own little apartment. Right before the babies came home, Alex had, in a fit of anxiety, the basement converted into an ultra-modern apartment for Lily while also rigging the whole apartment up with intercoms. On top of that, both our room and Lily's bedroom had full-screen monitors that showed the nursery 24/7.

Alex and I switch off on baby bath duty. He entertains Jasper and feeds him a few more ounces of formula before bed while I gently wash Jasmine. Even after she had come off of the feeding tube, I found myself being extra gentle with her like she was made of fine china. She babbles while I shampoo her tiny hair tufts, splashing excitedly, but the soothing lavender scent of the baby wash begins to work its magic and she's quiet and droopy-eyed when I pull her out and wrap her in a fluffy white towel.

Alex passes me with Jasper cradled in his arms as I leave the bathroom. Jasper wriggles like a fish in his dad's arms when he sees me and his sister, and I wish Alex luck as I take little Jasmine to the nursery to put her to bed. I dress her in a soft flannel sleep sack and by the time I lay her down, humming as I do so, she's completely out, her tiny arms stretched above her head in slumber.

I check her ankle monitor one final time before turning the lights out. The little pink ankle band monitors her breathing and heart rate, reporting any inconsistencies straight to our phones. We had also placed a movement monitor underneath the sheets of their cribs. If Alex had the choice, he would probably have hired a whole nursing staff to be on hand, but the monitors offered us enough peace of mind that we could sleep without worry.

As I go to leave the room, Alex enters, Jasper fighting a losing battle against sleep in his arms. Jasper is dry and wrapped in a fluffy towel of his own, but Alex looks like he had just finished swimming in the ocean, the chest of his shirt soaked through.

"He's wild tonight," Alex comments exhaustedly, causing me to laugh.

"I guess I should've warned you," I tell him, kissing him and Jasper both on the cheeks before leaving Alex to put his son to bed.

I'm sitting on the bed unbraiding my hair when Alex comes back, jerking his wet shirt over his head and throwing it into the laundry basket. I blink a few times, taking in my husband's toned body and the dark shadow of stubble on his jaw.

"Shower?" he asks me. "I'm already halfway there, thanks to our son."

I consider the proposition. I palm the outline of my phone in my pocket, thinking about sending Nico Tucci another text before bed but ultimately deciding against it. After all, Alex is half-naked, and the twins are both asleep. This doesn't happen often.

I recline back on my elbows, looking him over. "I don't know, babe. I'm pretty exhausted," I tease.

"Get your mind out of the gutter," he shoots back with a smirk. "All I said was a shower. Nothing more. It'll be warm and relaxing."

A snort rolls off my lips at his tone. "Fiiiine," I groan dramatically, sliding off the bed. Then I throw my own shirt off as I lead the way to our enormous shower. "So that means you are gonna keep your hands to yourself?" I ask jokingly.

Alex's laugh is deep and seductive behind me as I turn the steaming water on. "I didn't say that."

Sleep doesn't come, no matter how much I toss and turn. Alex lays next to me, the sound of his breathing a comfort that should have helped lull me into slumber, but for some reason, I just can't get there.

I roll to my side again, sighing and scrunching my eyes shut. *Come on, just fall asleep already!*

One of the things you hear most as a pregnant woman is the idea that *"you need to sleep when the baby sleeps."* It made sense when I was still pregnant, but once I had given birth, I realized how absurd that idea was.

For starters, newborns sleep in fits and starts. Five minutes here, an hour there, but never long enough. That type of sleep schedule just doesn't work for adults. Nothing is less restful than a five-minute nap interrupted by a screaming infant. My experience had been different from most, with the extended stay in the NICU, but it wasn't like that allowed for a restful experience either.

The nurses, bless their souls, had tried to herd me back to my hospital room constantly. My cesarean had gone off without a hitch, making it somehow one of the less stressful moments of my pregnancy up to that point, but it was still invasive surgery, and I needed to heal. I did try to rest, lying flat so my incision could heal, but more often than not I was pulling on grippy hospital socks and shuffling painfully down to the twins' NICU suite. I couldn't stay away.

That was almost five months ago, and most of the time I sleep like a log, but there are still times like this one that I'm too restless, kept awake by my racing thoughts. But now, it wasn't worry for Jasmine and Jasper on my mind, but rather it was my enchantment with The Artemis Room gallery. I am trying not to obsess… and am failing miserably.

I have memories of that place from when I was a little girl, looking up at the artwork and wondering if I would ever be that talented, and then even more memories from my teenage years, when I would walk the halls by myself, basking in the serene silence of the place. It seems almost blasphemous for a place that had brought me so much peace to become a bar or a restaurant. The thought alone causes a shiver of distaste to roll along my spine.

Alex feels my shiver, rolls over, and cracks open his eyes to look at me. His eyes, deep blue from sleepiness, take in the tightness of my mouth and the tension in my jaw. He sits up with a groan. "Can't sleep?"

I shake my head. "Too much on my mind."

He looks sympathetic, scooting closer to me and letting me pillow my head on his lap while he strokes my hair. "Anything that I can help you with? Baby stuff? House stuff?"

"No," I assure him. "Just a lot of thoughts about the gallery, is all. I'm trying not to get my hopes up but every time I close my eyes I imagine how I would set the place up, which paintings I would put where, and what new artists to feature." A sigh escapes me. "I know I'm setting myself up for disappointment, but I just can't help it."

Alex ponders my words for a moment, before sliding out of bed. "I'll be right back."

I watch curiously as he pulls on a pair of sweatpants and a sweatshirt, leaving the bedroom. I snuggle back under the down comforter, missing his warmth already. Whatever he's doing, he takes his time with it, and had it been any other night I'd be snoozing peacefully by the time he got back. Instead, I'm still wide awake, tracking him with my eyes when he returns.

He pulls my velour robe off of the hook on the back of our bedroom door and tosses it to me. "Put that on and follow me."

"Alex, what—" I start, but he's already disappeared into the dark house. I scowl, slipping the robe over my shoulders and following him.

I tie the belt around my waist, looking around for my husband to no avail. Finally, I see a flickering light coming from the terrace, different from the static lights of the city. I walk to the glass doors and glance out, spotting Alex.

He's lit a fire in the terra cotta chiminea and pulled our outdoor wicker loveseat close, lounging on the padded couch in the firelight. He sees me at the door and waves me over. I consider turning around and going back to bed, but with a resigned sigh I open the doors and slip out.

Despite the terrace being insulated, the poured concrete floor is freezing cold for the first few steps, and I tiptoe to minimize skin contact until I'm closer to the chiminea. About three feet away I can feel the heat radiating, and once I make it to the loveseat with Alex, I'm not frigid anymore. If I'm being honest, it may even be a little toasty in my velour robe.

Alex pulls me close when I sit down, and I tuck my feet underneath me for warmth as I fit myself against him. We watch the fire burn in silence, until I finally ask, "Why exactly are we doing this?"

"I thought some fresh air might help soothe your mind," he says quietly, gazing into the fire.

It certainly is cozy. With all the light pollution from the city, we can't see many stars, but the icy breeze mixed with the blooming warmth of the outdoor fireplace combine perfectly to make our own little paradise in a sea of cold weather. The wood crackles, filling the quiet air over the noise of the city beyond.

Alex throws a fleece blanket over us both, and the experience of watching the fire is almost meditative. He slips a hand under my robe to drag his knuckles up and down my bare arm, lost in thought. I can tell his mind is elsewhere from the distant look in his eyes.

"Something on your mind?" I ask in a hushed tone.

"Just mulling over some business plans in my head, that's all," he says.

"Anything important?"

He gazes at me fondly, tenderness written all over his features. "Pretty important, yeah. Kind of a spur-of-the-moment thing I have to throw together."

"Sounds stressful."

"Hopefully not," Alex sighs. "Only time will tell."

As the minutes pass us by in companionable silence, I feel my eyelids getting heavy against all odds. Here beneath the night sky is the last place I imagined I would find rest tonight, but with my head on Alex's shoulder, I doze off into a deep, dreamless sleep, wrapped in the warmth of the fire and my husband's arms.

I don't even wake up when he carries me to bed, nearly an hour later.

CHAPTER 3

Manhattan, November 19, 2021
Petra

I'm sleeping deeply when the sound of the bedroom door opening cuts through my slumber. Groaning, I throw my arm over my face, hoping that I'm dreaming and it's really still the middle of the night, but whoever has disturbed me doesn't stop. I hear the pulling of curtains, and a beam of bright sunlight cuts across my face.

"Noooo…" I mumble, pulling a pillow over my face, but Maria clucks and opens the curtains wider.

"I'm sorry, ma'am, but it's time to wake up," she tells me.

I crack my eyes open and look at her. She's standing with her hands on her hips, looking both amused and exasperated. I roll over to glance at the clock on the bedside. It reads nine a.m. Well, crap. I guess I really do need to get up.

"The twins?" I ask her, stretching my arms over my head with an enormous yawn.

"Lily got them up at six o'clock and fed them some formula," she responds, bustling around the room to gather the dirty laundry. "She also suggested that you start giving them some dry cereal now that they are close to five months old."

"And where's Alex?"

Maria sighs. "He has to go into work again today and would like it if you two have breakfast together before he leaves."

"Alright, alright," I complain, reluctantly getting out of bed. Alex and I had stayed up a little later than anticipated last night, both with our joint shower and fireside nap. I thought I would catch a few extra moments of sleep before I had to face the day. Oh well.

My hair is mussed from being slept on while wet, so I pull a brush through it after brushing my teeth and getting ready for the day. Alex is dressed for work, his suit jacket draped over the back of the chair when I come in. His beard is freshly trimmed, and the ivory of his shirt complements his tan complexion. I lean down for a quick kiss and take my seat, grasping the steaming mug of matcha tea that is waiting for me.

"Good morning, Sleeping Beauty," Alex comments with a smirk over the rim of his coffee cup.

"Same to you, Prince Charming," I reply, matching his tone and giving him a flirtatious wink. "Where are the babies?"

"Lily is getting them dressed. She'll be right back. Something about wanting you to try and feed them some rice cereal this morning?"

"Yeah," I mumble vaguely. "I know I shouldn't be, but I'm still so apprehensive about feeding solids to Jasmine. I think Jasper could polish off some avocado toast if we let him, but it still feels like just yesterday our little Jas had a feeding tube. Lily knows I'm nervous, so she's pressing the issue whether I like it or not," I explain, popping a grape from the fruit selection on the table in my mouth and chewing thoughtfully.

Alex hesitates, setting his coffee cup on the table. "Is she sure Jasmine is ready for solids?"

"Lily suggested just a little bit at a time to get started as Jasmine needs the calories to grow." I swirl my tea in my mug as I continue, "What if something goes wrong though?"

Alex looks ready to respond, but Lily returns with the twins just then, one perched on each hip. Carrying them both is something I'm still trying to master. We have multiple chest carriers, the traditional kind, and the baby-wearing variety, but they swiftly give me backache every time I'd tried to use them. Alex, being taller and stronger, has a little more success with them, but neither of us feels totally comfortable having tiny Jasmine in the traditional variety. She does better in the baby sling, tucked close to our chests.

Lily, on the other hand, carries them both without a carrier like it's the easiest thing in the world. I pop out of my chair and take Jasper, kissing his face before depositing him in his high chair, and strapping him in. Lily gets Jasmine into her chair, which is bigger than Jasper's, offering more support for her little body. Both of them know what the chairs mean, and are huffing excitedly, kicking their legs and waving their arms.

Lily had been in charge of the slow introduction of rice cereal to Jasper, but I still had so much anxiety about doing the same with Jasmine. I chew a few more grapes while Lily goes to prepare the cereal.

Alex checks his watch. "I've got a few minutes. I'll stay and give you ladies a hand."

"Thanks," I tell him, watching as he stands to roll up his sleeves.

Lily returns and hands us each a small bowl with a few spoonfuls of the beige, pasty cereal inside. "Small bites, and make sure their mouths are completely empty before their next bite. At this age, they'll have their mouths open for the next bite before they've even swallowed the first, so just be careful."

Jasper nearly screams when Alex scoops some of the cereal into the soft rubber spoon and guides it to his mouth. "Patience, little man! We'll get there!" Alex jokes, feeding Jasper with no sign of the nerves that I am currently experiencing.

Jasmine is still kicking, looking between me and the bowl. I can tell she's gearing up for a loud protest if I don't hurry it up, but all I can do is stir the cereal to stall.

"Go ahead, Petra," Lily encourages. "She's hungry."

Steeling myself, I scoop up barely half a spoon of cereal and hold it to Jasmine's pursed lips. She opens her mouth like a little bird, and excitedly accepts the spoons when I give her a bite, gumming the cereal with a serious look on her face.

I'm so afraid she's going to choke that I don't breathe until I visibly see her swallow, opening her mouth again expectantly. I blow out a relieved breath and chuckle nervously, feeding her the next bite. She smiles hugely, all gums, and laughs along with me after she finishes the second bite.

"Amazing job, both of you!" Lily congratulates.

"You don't think I'm silly for being so nervous about feeding my own daughter, do you?" I ask her.

She shakes her head. "Absolutely not. Everything you do with them is a first for you. Trust me when I say every parent second guesses themselves the entire way through."

The sense of triumph I feel when I scrape the bottom of the cereal bowl is ridiculous for such a minor task, but I mentally pat myself on the back, anyway. Maria clears our breakfast away and Alex shrugs his jacket on with a sigh.

"I have to go now, I promised your dad I'd attend this meeting with him," he says, tapping each baby on their button nose before kissing me goodbye. "I'll see you all for dinner?"

"Of course," I respond, walking him to the door. Once we stand alone by the entryway, I help him put on his winter peacoat, and then lowering my voice, I ask, "Did he talk to you about me?"

Alex doesn't seem surprised at my question; after all, he knows exactly what I'm talking about. "Well, you know your dad," he answers vaguely. "Don't worry, he'll get over it."

"He hasn't returned my calls, though."

"Give him some time," Alex insists, trying to appease me. "He just learned last week that his one and only daughter hasn't been attending classes this semester. For him, that's like the end of the world."

I nod, knowing there isn't much I can do at this point. Dad can be stubborn just like me. I pull on the lapels of the coat to bring Alex closer to me, kissing him one more time. "I'll miss you," I murmur against his lips.

"I'll miss you too, wife," he responds warmly.

I release my husband reluctantly. Once he shuts the door behind him, I'm left standing alone, wondering what to make of my day. Emma and I had discussed doing some early Christmas shopping for the twins. Alex would willingly hire a decorator to make the condo festive for us, but with it being the babies' first Christmas, I really wanted Emma and me to do it ourselves. Plus, I know she loves this kind of stuff.

But there's a shadow looming over me I can't shake, and it's my powered-down phone sitting on the charger in the bedroom. Once I turned it on, I would either have a response from Nico, or I'd have to touch base with him and potentially face rejection. As long as the phone remained turned off, I could stay in the dark about whether or not he had decided to sell to me.

Yesterday I had been so full of cocky confidence on the phone with Nico, but the longer without an answer I go, the more nervous I become. I have to face the music and talk to him again today, whether or not I want to. After talking to Alex last night, I realize it has been a mistake for my first real estate purchase to be something emotionally significant to me. It'd have been easier to buy something that wasn't anything but a professionally beneficial purchase, instead of something I really cared about. Oh well, too late now.

Lily is cleaning the babies' faces off when I return to them. "Anything special on the agenda today?" she asks me, and I chew my lip for a moment before responding.

"I was going to go shopping with Emma for some Christmas decorations for the condo, maybe a new tree," I respond, but my heart isn't in it.

Lily examines my expression for a moment.

"You're looking conflicted. Do you need to go do something while I finish cleaning these two up?" she asks gently.

I close my eyes for a moment before nodding. "Yeah, if you don't mind. I need to make some phone calls."

"Go ahead!" Lily says. "I'll take them to the nursery to play and work on some movement exercises."

"Thanks, Lily," I say, relieved and full of anxiety all at the same time.

I retrieve my phone from the bedside table and toss it back and forth between my hands, thinking everything over. Somehow trying to brace myself for what is to come. Eventually, I decided to go to our home office to make the call. Maybe I will be in a more professional mindset if I have the right environment.

Our home office is a dark forest green with equally dark oak flooring. The desk is old, antique even, and as I come to think of it, it fits Alex's personality; strong, stoic, and unmovable. Light filters in through the open blinds, lightening up the heavy, somber room. I sink into the rolling leather chair and power my phone on, tapping my fingers nervously on the desk as I wait.

The screen lights up, and for a minute my text inbox is empty. I nearly jump out of my skin when a message comes through, but my adrenaline rapidly dies down when I see it's just Emma.

"*We still on for Christmas shopping?*" her message reads. I text her back an affirmative.

Scrolling through my email, texts, and voicemails reveals nothing. Nico still hasn't messaged me. I guess that means I'll have to make the first move.

"*Good morning, Mr. Tucci. This is Petra Van Gatt, checking up on the offer I extended to you regarding The Artemis Room yesterday afternoon.*"

I read over the text a few times, debating on adding anything else. Finally, I finish it off with, "*I'll be looking at some other galleries today, so please get back to me as soon as possible. Thank you.*"

Hitting send, I pocket my phone again with a sigh. Maybe if Nico knows that I'm in the market for other galleries, it will light a fire under him to get back to me sooner. I know the clock is ticking, and he could very well have sold the building already without telling me. Maybe I really should check out some other places to ease my mind.

I dial Emma's number, and she picks up on the third ring.

"Hey," I begin. "Can we make a few pit stops before we go Christmas shopping?"

Emma hums on the other line for a moment, thinking over my proposition, before answering, "Sure, I've got nothing else planned today anyway."

"Great. I'll see you soon."

With quick fingers, I switch on the Mac and access a few of the local business real estate websites, printing out pages upon pages of available office spaces. Not all of them would be suited to include a gallery, but if push comes to shove, then I could have separate spaces. Ideally though, I would have one building that could do both. I didn't want my future employees to be too disconnected from the artwork and the artists themselves. My fund wouldn't be simply business. We had to connect with the actual people, hearing what they needed most from us to succeed in a difficult art world.

Once I'm finished, I recline back in the leather office chair, looking around the office that had been Alex's before I'd moved in, and start envisioning what I would like my own office to look like. It would be brighter, with more open windows and sunlight. I would cover the walls with my favorite pieces of art that I've done over the years and some from other artists I love. Soon enough, I would have my own space. Whether it be The Artemis Room, or not.

But gosh, I really wanted it to be The Artemis Room.

CHAPTER 4

Petra

Emma and I hustle back to the car, jumping into the back seat before Zach can even consider opening the doors for us. The weather is overcast, not quite raining, but misty and cold enough for it to be unpleasant.

Emma rubs her bare hands together and blows into them for warmth while I shuffle through my packet of buildings that are for sale, crossing another potential off with a red pen. I exhale in annoyance, flipping through the pages.

"I'm going to assume that one was a resounding no, right?" Emma asks, tucking her icy hands into her leather coat pockets.

"The bottom floor was a doggy daycare, Emma! Not exactly conducive to artistic expression!" I rant, causing Emma to giggle.

"I don't know, dogs are pretty inspiring, don't you think?" she cajoles.

"You must be joking. I'm going to just assume that you aren't being serious because if I had to run any kind of business with all that yapping, I'd go absolutely insane in the first hour." I toss my packet of papers on the leather middle seat between Emma and me with a sigh. "The next option is over ten miles away..."

"In that case," she says, "we should stop real estate hunting and go Christmas shopping! You know, as we had originally planned?"

Emma and I had visited five different potential galleries and offices at this point, and we had been on the hunt for over three hours. She's always a good sport, humoring me and giving her honest opinion on each space we visited. I knew this wasn't exactly the type of shopping Emma had agreed to, but I was still thankful for her support.

The first option had been close to my condo, and on paper, it checked all the boxes. It was an office building with a finished basement that could easily be turned into a gallery. The offices themselves were large and open, there was a built-in kitchenette, and a fantastic amount of parking. The only problem was that the building was smack in the middle of an industrial park, surrounded by some of the most boring businesses known to man, and worst of all, it was boring. Painfully boring, even. The only signage allowed was clingfilm on the glass windows. It honestly just wasn't going to work.

Next was a two-floor rental in one of the downtown high-rises, and while a shared building wasn't ideal, the location was very accessible. I could have made it work, except the ad for the rental failed to mention that it was on two totally separate floors: the 3rd and the 26th. Not sure what they were thinking with that one.

The third option was my favorite of the bunch. It was an old one-room school building that had been recently renovated with modern windows, flooring, and roofing. It was a gorgeous piece of history that would have suited my needs perfectly for the gallery portion, even if I would need to house the office elsewhere. I had felt my first twinge of excitement until the real estate agent took us to the basement, and we all discovered that a vandal had stripped all the copper piping, doing thousands of dollars of damage in the process.

And fourth, right before the doggy daycare fiasco, was an industrial warehouse. Spaces like this, with visible pipes and beams, were all the rage right now, and although it would have needed some serious drywall work to add in restrooms and offices, the price was just right. The agent had unlocked the door when Emma suddenly grabbed my arm.

"I have a bad feeling about this one," she had said, uncertainty in her eyes.

We stepped back, and the agent shrugged, agreeing to go in first. He was chased out seconds later by angry squatters that had claimed the old warehouse for their own.

It had been an utter disaster.

I still wanted to keep looking, but after the agent who was showing us the last building had to pause the tour to scoop up an errant senior chihuahua that had escaped the daycare in the middle of our appointment, I was officially over it.

"Okay, okay, you win," I tell her. "Where do you want to go?"

Emma looks at the driver through the rearview mirror and says, "Zach? Let's head to Macy's."

"Yes, ma'am," he answers over his shoulder before pulling out into traffic.

"Eek! I'm so excited, aren't you? I bet Alex has all the usual stuffy Christmas decorations in storage. We're gonna make sure these babies have the most fabulous, sparkliest Christmas ever!" Emma gushes, her tone dripping with joy.

I wouldn't admit it to Emma, but she was sort of right—Alex's Christmas decorations are actually nonexistent. After all, we had spent last Christmas in the Netherlands, so we'd never bothered to buy anything for the condo. But not having a proper decorated home is the last thing I want for Jasmine and Jasper's Christmas.

I didn't want classy white lights on a green tree. I wanted a riot of colors. Golds, silvers, and lights of all the colors of the rainbow. Something for the twins to look at and be entertained. Something magical. We deserved it after the last year.

I can already hear Alex now, giving his usual sense of taste, "*Petra, it's overkill. It looks ridiculous in here.*" But I knew he would change his tune as soon as he saw the lights reflected in the babies' eyes.

"I'm shocked that you're this excited about Christmas. I thought you would want a dead tree with a raven on top of something," I joke, and she scowls at me.

"Haha, hilarious. It's gonna be my godchildren's first Christmas," she says, her tone filled with enthusiasm. "I want it to be epic."

I laugh and she reluctantly joins in. Emma may prefer leather jackets, tattoos, and dark cherry lipsticks, but she had two weaknesses: the holidays, and more recently, the twins. When it came to those things, her tough persona flew out the window entirely and she was full of whimsy. It's why she asked me to go shopping with her.

Sure, it was still November, but Thanksgiving was such a boring holiday to decorate for. Halloween had been fun, but the twins were still too young to take trick or treating. Instead, though, we dressed them up and let friends and family come to us. Jasper had been the cowardly lion from The Wizard of Oz, his chubby face adorable in the furry mane hood of his costume jumper, and Jasmine had been Dorothy, wearing a knit hat with two yarn braids hanging off the side and a blue checkered dress. Of course, she had tugged and fussed with the fake braids from the get-go, so we decided Dorothy would be bald, discarding the hat with a laugh.

No candy, of course, although my dad had covertly slid a king-sized pack of peanut butter cups into my hand before he left. As I come to think of it, maybe I should give him another call. It has been a week since I told him I wasn't attending Columbia this semester, meaning it had been a week since he stopped talking to me. The shock on his face when I told him I'd resume college only in January isn't something easy to forget. Plus in only a few days it's Thanksgiving and I have no idea if Dad is coming over or not.

Emma is all but glowing when we pull up to Macy's, and for some reason, I'm pretty psyched myself. The city hasn't quite yet transformed into the winter wonderland it'd become the day after Thanksgiving, but it's still beautiful, the warm colors of fall broken up here and there with the glittering red, green, and silver of Christmas.

As we step in, Emma asks the security guard something, while I take in my surroundings. I have been here only once before and had totally forgotten how enormous this department store is. There are a lot of people around, and it feels quite chaotic. Geez, only Emma would want to bring me to Macy's.

"Santaland is on the eighth floor, but it doesn't officially start until the 27th," Emma informs me as we head towards the escalators. "I'm sure that's where the decorations are, though."

"Damn, I was so looking forward to taking a picture of you on Santa's lap," I tease with a grin.

"It will have to wait a few weeks, unfortunately," Emma sarcastically replies, patting me on the arm.

The eighth floor still features Thanksgiving decorations, but more than half of it has already been switched over to Christmas. When we step off the escalator, I have to turn in a circle to take it all in. While I have been to this Macy's once before, I've never been here intending to buy Christmas decor for an entire condo.

"Did you make a list?" Emma asks.

"Uh… no," I grimace, but she seems unperturbed.

"Free for all it is. Let's start with the tree!" Emma takes my hand and rushes me over to the trees, excitement written all over her face.

Her happiness is infectious, and before I know it, I'm just as joyful, letting the stress of The Artemis Room slip away for at least a little while.

* * *

The sales representative, a middle-aged woman in a crisp black pantsuit, taps her pen on her clipboard a few times as she goes over my purchases. She clicks the pen and makes a few notations before tucking it back into her lapel pocket.

"We can have everything delivered Monday around midday. Will that be suitable for you, Ms. Van Gatt?"

"Absolutely," I reply. The wait would allow me time to break it gently to Alex that I had spent an obscene amount of money on Christmas decor and other silly things.

"That will give you time to find space to store all of this!" Emma teases, gesturing to the items the sales rep has marked with the delivery date.

Emma and I have a few bags clutched in our hands, but the tree and other items of my larger order would need to be delivered. It would never fit in the back of the car.

"Hush, you," I tell her, waving her away.

The sales rep hands me her clipboard and I sign where she indicates, completing the purchase. I take a last look at my haul before heading out of the store with Emma at my side. Zach is waiting for us out front, the trunk wide open. We hand him our bags and settle into the car. I'm all smiles, and Emma notices.

"Feeling better?" she asks, and I nod.

"For sure," I answer, fighting the urge to check my phone.

We have been gone a long portion of the day, and I was starting to miss the twins. Lily had called earlier in the afternoon to let me know they were having a nap, but they would most likely be awake by now.

Emma follows me into the condo, and we shuck our outerwear, hanging them on the coat rack.

I offer her a drink, but she declines. I know she only has one thing on her mind now that we're back home: the twins. We cross the hallway and get into the nursery, a bright and airy room with just the slightest color accents here and there. Lily is sitting in the rocking chair in the corner, watching the twins play.

Jasmine is in a bouncer, surrounded by brightly colored, obnoxiously loud toys that she is studiously ignoring. Jasper is loose, his pudgy hands gripping the side of Jasmine's bouncer. It's good standing practice for him, and he's slapping at a red rubber flower when Jasmine takes offense, pushing his hand away so she can manhandle the flower toy herself.

Jasper sticks his bottom lip out, falling to his butt. He is moments away from crying, incensed that he had his toy taken away when Emma scoops him up. She tickles his sides and rubs her nose against his, and his tears clear up immediately.

"What's up, little man? Getting bullied by your sister already?" Emma asks him, sitting down on the floor with Jasper and plonking him down in front of her.

Jasper babbles in response, crawling right back into Emma's lap. She lets him, stroking his hair absentmindedly as he snuggles up to her, content to play with the stuffed elephant she plucks off the floor and hands to him.

"Did you get everything accomplished you set out to do?" Lily asks.

"Yes, and then some," I tell her, sitting down heavily in one of the plush reading chairs against the wall.

"I'm exhausted," Emma says, rolling her eyes to the ceiling, "I must be getting old if shopping is wearing me out so much."

"Oh, stop, you know—" I'm cut off when my phone, deep within the purse I had discarded on the floor next to me, pings with a message.

I dig through the purse excitedly, feeling a strange mixture of hopefulness and dread. I touch the familiar metal shape of my phone and pull it out, unlocking my screen and pulling up the message. It's from Alex. Deflating a little when I see the sender, I open the message anyway.

"Hello, my beautiful wife. I'm running a bit late. I have an unexpected meeting I can't miss. I took the initiative to order pizza for you and Emma. You should have a movie night. I'll join you when I get off work. Love you."

A smile flits across my face at the sweet message, dulling some of the disappointment I was feeling from still not having heard from Nico. The time on my phone reads 5:45 pm, and suddenly my stomach growls loudly, causing both babies to laugh and Emma and Lily to raise their eyebrows.

"Stop looking at me like that!" I joke, hiding my face behind my hands before popping back out, earning another round of giggles from the twins. "Emma, want to stay for dinner and a movie? Alex ordered us some pizza. He said he'd be late."

She considers it while Jasper tries his best to reach her shoulder-length, glossy black hair, before nodding. "Sounds good. What are we watching?"

"Oh! I've got an idea. Why don't we invite Matt? He's always got the best off-the-wall movies," I suggest.

Emma looks intrigued, and she opens her mouth like she's about to protest, but instead simply shrugs, agreeing to it. I start to get excited about the prospect of a low-key movie night with my best friends, who just so happen to also be the twins' godparents. I shoot Alex a text, letting him know Matt would be coming, before sending Emma out to prepare the living room for maximum movie viewing comfort while Lily and I prepare the twin's dinner bottles.

"Ask Maria to pop some popcorn for us too!" I yell at Emma's back as she leaves the nursery, and she throws me a thumbs up.

I snap a quick picture of Jasmine, looking particularly adorable in a dove gray romper, and text it to Matt with the caption, *"Your favorite goddaughter cordially invites you to a movie night at her mother's condo. Bring a cool flick, nothing too lame."*

Minutes later, he responds, accepting the invitation with a list of potential movies. He has a rare, supposedly nonexistent director's cut of a famous superhero movie, so I tell him to bring that one, not being in the mood for any serious documentaries.

I'm almost giddy while Lily and I speed run the babies' baths and dinner, dressing them in matching hooded sleepers, Jasmine's a panda and Jasper's a grizzly bear. It's early for their baths, and they're both droopy-eyed when we dry them off, but with a few tickles they're wide awake again and ready to join the grown-ups for the movie, at least for a little while.

A huge grin blooms on my face when I carry Jasmine out to the living room. Emma has outdone herself, and I'm shocked Maria allowed her so much control. The couch has been pushed back a few feet and loaded up with blankets, but she has also made what could only be called a floor bed in front of the couch.

Emma had spread comforters and pillows out to make a huge space for her and me to lie with the twins while we watch the movie, an enormous bowl of buttery popcorn resting on the table next to the floor bed. It looks like a high school slumber party, and I am so here for it.

Matt had arrived while I had been finishing up with the little ones, and was reclined on the couch, having correctly guessed that he wasn't invited to the floor bed with Emma and me. He sits up when I walk in, holding his arms out expectantly. I hand him Jasmine with a smirk, and he takes her gently, holding her close as he looks her up and down.

"You're growing too fast. I can't keep up!" he tells her seriously, fighting back a smile when she screeches at him in response. He gives her a quick peck on the nose before handing her back to me and calling out, "Next baby, please!"

Matt makes a big show of struggling under Jasper's weight when Lily hands him over, causing Jasper to cackle in laughter. "What have they been feeding you, entire hams?" Matt asks his godson, who declines to respond, instead mussing Matt's tousled hair with his little hands.

Emma, in true best friend fashion, had apparently gone into my bedroom and changed into some of my pajamas, this pair being navy blue and covered in tiny white snowflakes. "Nice get up," I tell her, sitting down on the blankets with her, and she snorts.

"Like I was supposed to watch a movie and eat pizza in a Gucci leather coat and jeans? Get real," she tells me, reaching over me and grabbing a handful of popcorn.

After some catching up with Matt, we finally start the movie, Jasper spending the entire time with Matt and Jasmine making her rounds between Emma, Lily, and me. We turn the lights out, and with our enormous TV lighting up the room, it almost feels like a real theater.

The pizza shows up a bit later. We pause the movie, and while I grab plates for everyone, the babies get passed around the group for goodnight kisses before Lily takes them up to the nursery so everyone can eat.

"I can't believe how big they've gotten," Matt comments between bites of pizza.

"You should come by more often, then it wouldn't be so much of a surprise," I respond, giving him a pointed look.

He rubs the back of his neck before responding. "Ah, yeah, I know. I've just been so busy between college, my YouTube channel, and Sarah." *Wow.* They are still together? Not that I thought they couldn't have a serious long-term relationship, but it's still impressive that it's working out for the two of them.

"Fair enough," I say with a shrug.

Lily comes back after a while, snagging a few slices of pizza before heading to her apartment. Matt, Emma, and I are so engrossed in the action movie that when, a little more than halfway through the movie, Alex arrives home we all jump; he looks all of us over with an amused expression.

"I'll be right back. Just let me go change," he says, shaking his head as he goes.

When Alex gets back, he settles onto the floor behind me, letting me pillow my head in his lap.

"I checked on Jasmine and Jasper," he tells me, his voice low so as to not disturb the others. "They're knocked out. What do you say after this movie is over you kick those two out and we," he pitches his voice even lower, adding in a little bit of growl, "make our own entertainment?"

I blush, thankful for the darkened room, and pinch his thigh. "Shh!" I hiss.

He chuckles. "I'll take that as a yes."

Emma looks over at us as we kiss and mouths the word "Gross," at me, and I struggle not to giggle.

Alex cards his hands gently through my hair as the movie continues, and I find myself humming contentedly.

On the screen, one of the heroes has toppled off a cliff and everyone is on edge, myself included, so when my cellphone, which I had placed on the coffee table, pings with a message, we all startle. I sit up, laughing nervously and holding my hand to my chest.

"Emma, can you pause the movie so I can go check that?" I ask self-consciously.

"Sure, doll." Emma sits up, fumbling for the remote that Matt eventually hands her, and clicks the pause button.

I find my phone in the dark, squinting from the bright light of the screen. I thumb the messaging app open, seeing a message from an unsaved number. My pulse jumps. Could it be Nico? I click it and read it so fast I have to go over it twice.

"Good evening, Ms. Van Gatt. I wanted to inform you that the building has officially been sold and is off the market. Thank you for your interest. Cheers, Nico"

My heart drops to my feet, and I exhale a shuddering breath as I try to collect myself. Misery, real and palpable, floods me, and I just want to pull the blanket over my head and hide. My distress must have been obvious, because Alex, with a concerned look on his face, lays his hand on my knee.

"What's up? Is everything okay?" he asks softly.

I rub my eyes, hoping to avoid any tears. "Yeah, I'm fine. That was the owner of The Artemis Room. He's sold the building."

"Oh Petra, I'm sorry," Emma says, her tone empathetic and her eyebrows drawn together.

Matt's mouth tightens sympathetically. "Was that the gallery Emma mentioned earlier? That's harsh, P. I can look into some other places if you want. I've got a buddy in school whose dad gets early tips from the local real estate agents and—"

"It's nothing..." I try to convince them, even though I feel like crying. "There are other places. It's totally fine."

"Hmm," Emma responds, sounding unconvinced.

"Seriously, let's just finish the movie. What's done is done," I tell them.

Alex is strangely silent but gives me a reassuring squeeze on the knee. After looking a bit more convincing, we restart the movie. I can't focus on it, of course, but I sit silently beside Alex for the remainder of the film, eventually laying my head on his shoulder and planning some sort of plan B as everyone else leaves.

I try to pay attention to the rest of the movie, laughing on cue at Emma and Matt's quirky commentary, but it's a huge relief when the credits begin to roll. I stand up and stretch, trying not to count the seconds until I'm alone and can pout to my heart's content.

Matt and Alex end up conversing about something out of earshot, and I walk Emma to the door after she grabs her things. She shrugs on her coat but pauses with her hand on the doorknob. "You want your pajamas back?" she asks, pulling at the flannel pajama pants.

I shake my head, trying to grin jokingly. "It's okay, I know where you live if I need them badly enough," I just answer with a quick shrug.

Emma's gaze softens, and she takes her hand off of the doorknob, wrapping me in a hug. "I know that gallery meant something to you, babe. Don't give up. You'll find something better, or maybe that new restaurant will bomb and close in a year or two. All isn't lost."

I let myself melt into her embrace, the warmth of her friendship helping to ease the ache of disappointment inside of me. "You really think so?" I ask, sounding more vulnerable than I expected.

"This is nothing compared to what you've been through. Everything will work out, maybe in ways you never expected." She squeezes me tightly once more before letting go. "Call me tomorrow?"

I nod, and she leaves with a wave. I glance over at Alex and Matt, and right at that moment, Matt gives me a silly grin before turning back to Alex and talking animatedly. Alex looks mildly amused at the younger man's enthusiasm, and my interest is immediately piqued. What could they be talking about? These two don't have much in common, but they seem to be discussing something important. Whatever, I guess I don't really care, as long as they are getting along.

Maria must have turned in early, so I pick up the pizza boxes and metal popcorn bowl, depositing them on the kitchen counter for the morning. The condo has that certain intimate atmosphere that only comes late at night when I should be asleep. Everything is hushed, and I can even hear the faint sound of the fridge and some noise coming in from outside.

I hear Alex bidding Matt farewell as I brew myself a cup of lavender tea. He shuts the lights off in the rest of the condo, casting everywhere in shadow except the kitchen where I stand, clutching my mug.

My husband is gorgeous, but what else is new? His plain white t-shirt hugs every dip and curve of his chest, and his gray sweatpants are slung loosely on his trim waist. I'm sure that he had trimmed his beard before work, but at this time of night his jaw is shadowed with new stubble growth, and the vague sleepiness written on his face makes him even more handsome. In his element, suit and tie, perfectly coiffed hair, freshly trimmed face, and a carnivorous glint in his eyes, Alex is an almost untouchable sort of attractive. He is sharp, confident, and completely in control of everything, myself included. But here, barefoot and in comfortable clothes, Alex is a totally different sort of handsome. Warm, approachable, and yes… very touchable.

He's so sexy right now that I feel heat pooling in my belly, despite all the craziness that has happened today.

I take a long sip of my tea as he comes to me, sliding his hands up and down my arms when he reaches me. "Do you want to talk about it?"

"About what?" I ask coyly, wanting to replace the sadness inside of me with something a little more fun.

He brushes my cheek with his thumb, tracing the line of my cheekbone. "You know what, little Petra."

I finish my tea and set the cup on the marble counter with a click. Alex continues to trace the bones of my face and neck with his fingers and I return the favor, sliding my hands under his shirt to warm them on his skin. He's burning hot, the softness of his skin covering the hardness of his muscles.

"Don't get distracted," Alex rumbles, wrapping his hands around my wrists. "We need to talk about this, sweet wife."

My shoulders sag. "Fine. I feel awful. If I had just met Emma for lunch a week earlier, then maybe I could've gotten the jump on the building. Instead, I was too late. I wish I had never even known that it was for sale."

"So he really went ahead and sold it to that hospitality brand you told me about?" he asks, trying to catch up.

"He didn't specify, but who else would he have sold to? All he could say on the phone was convenience, convenience, convenience." I roll my eyes to the ceiling. "He probably would have sold it for a hundred dollars and a street hot dog if it was convenient enough for him."

Alex chuckles, his hands on my hips now, thumbs grazing my hipbones. "It all comes around. Let's give this loss some room to breathe, and then we'll get started on finding the perfect place. I think I might have a... knack for giving you exactly what you want." Alex draws closer to me with each word, eventually whispering into the shell of my ear and causing my skin to rise in goosebumps.

I gasp at the feeling of his hot breath, returning my hands to their previous path up his shirt and over the planes of his body. "Do you know exactly what I want right now? Since you have a knack, and all," I say shakily.

"In fact," he responds, his lips moving against the flesh of my neck as he kisses me there, "I do."

Without warning, Alex hauls me up with his hands wrapped around my waist and deposits me on the countertop. He plants a hand on either side of me, boxing me in with his tall body. Almost instinctually, I look up at him, and he slants his mouth over mine without a second thought.

Kissing Alex is like coming home, like a fire in the dead of winter, and like a bed with warm blankets and fresh sheets. When he is with me, and especially when he kisses me, I am surrounded by love.

And when he slips his tongue into my mouth, I am surrounded by something else too. Need.

"Alex," I breathe when he starts to work his way down my neck, jerking my shirt over my head and discarding it somewhere on the floor. His fingers make quick work of my bra, and before I know it, I'm completely topless right here on the kitchen counter, under the only light burning in a sea of darkness.

His hands don't go straight to my breasts. Instead, he strokes and caresses every inch of my arms, shoulders, neck, and stomach. Each touch is filled with more and more sensation until my body is buzzing with the electricity of it and little cries fall from my lips with each press of his fingers.

After what seems like an eternity, he rolls my nipples between his fingers, and I'm so overstimulated that the feeling shoots straight to my core so sharply that it almost seems like his hands are between my legs instead.

He makes a grunt of satisfaction and pushes his hands beneath me until he can shimmy my pants down my legs, followed by my panties. I shiver in the chill air, but he's back on me within seconds, warming me with the press of his body.

Alex whips his own shirt over his head, but when my seeking hands go to his waistband, he stops me. "No, I'm comforting you, remember?"

"But Alex–" I protest before he covers my mouth with his again.

He trails kisses down my collarbone, palming my tits until his mouth reaches first my right nipple, and then my left, mixing long sucks with tiny nips until I'm writhing on the hard marble counter.

By the time he finally pulls away, my nipples are hard and aching, and I can't even find any words as he lowers himself to his knees to put his head between my thighs. I moan at the erotic sight while Alex grasps my upper legs, his fingertips digging into my flesh.

"Was I right, my wife? Is that what you want?" he growls.

I wrack my brain for words, finally sputtering, "Yes, God, yes Alex."

The grin he gives me is wicked, and before I can take another breath, he licks between my folds, expertly finding my clit. I jump as if shocked, my back arching. I'm so wet and ready from his earlier ministrations that I can feel a climax building at the base of my spine almost immediately.

"Oh…" I whisper, and he holds me tighter when my hips buck unconsciously.

Alex licks and suckles on me, not too fast and not too slow, intent on driving me to a fast and furious orgasm. He had obviously finished teasing me, having worked my body into a frenzy, and all I can do to grip his hair between my fingers, my face tilted towards the sky as the telltale shivers start in my thighs.

I cry his name as the shivers turn into a wave, and I pant, grinding against Alex's face helplessly, the orgasm rolling through me hard. He never stops pleasuring me until it's over and I'm struggling to even sit straight, every bit of my energy gone and my brain feeling foggy.

Alex stands, a smug look on his face. He drags his forearm over his mouth. "Told you I know you," he gloats. I look up at him through my lashes, trying to catch my breath, and he laughs low in his throat before he scoops me up in his arms, carrying me toward our bedroom.

"I can walk," I insist, but Alex simply spanks my thigh where he's gripping me, causing me to yelp and fall silent. I guess I won't be walking.

He then tucks me under the covers of our bed, still completely nude. "I want to take care of *you*," I huff, before yawning hugely.

He places a finger on my lips, shushing me, and pushes my shoulder gently until I relent and lie down. My eyelids are so heavy, and I blink a few times, exhausted. I don't have to wait long for Alex to slide into the bed with me, pulling my body into his and wrapping me in his embrace.

"Feeling better?" he asks, voice soft.

"Mmhmm," I respond, reveling in the aftershocks of Alex's hard work. "I love you, you know."

He places a single kiss on my bare shoulder blade. "I love you too. Goodnight, little Petra."

CHAPTER 5

Manhattan, November 20, 2021
Petra

It's seven a.m., and for some reason, I'm wide awake. The twins aren't even up yet, but here I am. I wish my sleep schedule would settle into a rhythm again, but I guess it all happens in due time.

I'm not sure if it's the persistent sadness of losing The Artemis Room that woke me up, but now that I'm awake I'm restless, tossing and turning on our silk sheets while Alex snoozes away next to me, shirtless and only clad in his boxer briefs. I take some time to admire him in his slumber, his face serene and peaceful, the morning light gracing his body lovingly.

He's so handsome that it is distracting, and even after being married, I'm still struck by how lucky I am. Looking at him brings up something I've pushed into the back of my head though, an annoying little doubt that I've been trying to ignore.

I try to focus on other thoughts, but after a futile few minutes, I climb out of the bed with a resigned sigh and stand in front of the mirror over my vanity, turning this way and that to visually examine my body. Pregnancy hadn't changed me much at all, owing to my youth and good genetics. My hips are just a bit wider, and my boobs have kept a little bit of their extra size, but all in all, I looked pretty much the same.

Except for… the scar. I pull my nightgown up far enough to see my abdomen and the eight inch scar running along my bikini line. Most cesarean incisions were only between four and six inches long, but most people weren't delivering twins. Time had been of the essence, and the extra two inches didn't bother me much, but I'd be lying if I said I didn't have moments of seeing myself in the mirror after a shower while wincing. The scar just didn't seem like a part of me. It's bizarre that it's permanent.

"It just makes you more beautiful," a scratchy, sleepy voice says from the bed.

I meet Alex's gaze in the mirror. He's awoken and is sitting up against the headboard, one arm behind his head, watching me. "You have to say that," I quip. "You're my husband, you're morally obligated to."

"Even if I wasn't, it's a battle scar. Means you survived," he says. "Being a fighter like that makes you even more beautiful. You fought for our babies, remember?"

I let the hem of my gown go and fall back into place. "I'd take a million more scars for them, but that doesn't mean I have to *like* the scar."

"Well, I do like it. I think you will too, in time." He stretches and sits up fully, the blankets falling to his waist. "Your body is incredible, Petra. Stop your worrying."

I sigh. "It's hard to when yours is perfect, and mine isn't."

"Why don't you come back to bed and I'll show you how perfect it is," he says roughly, patting the bed next to him.

I turn my head and look at him over my shoulder. "You can't solve everything with sex."

He raises an eyebrow and smiles seductively. "But can I solve this with sex?"

I can't help but giggle and give in, slinking over to his side of the bed and straddling his lap. "I'm not sure, I guess I can let you give it a try."

He wraps his arms around me, pushing my gown up my thighs before pulling me flat on the bed with him, ignoring my laughs as he growls in my ear, "And try I will."

Before leaving the car, I read once more the message my dad sent me. Since Thanksgiving is in a few days, I'm thrilled to see he has put his pride aside and decided to invite us over— most likely at Alex's request, at least that is what I assume. After more than an entire week of not returning my calls, I'd have been the last person on earth to invite him over to spend Thanksgiving with us. Plus, I don't think I'd have had the mental fortitude to host it this year. Every day that passes means the twins are wilder, trying to sync their thoughts with their actions with variable success. It's adorable but having to make sure your child isn't eating whatever object they find on the floor is almost a full-time job, even with super nanny Lily on the case.

I reply a quick, *"Okay, thank you, see you soon,"* lock the phone and slip it back into my back pocket. Then I swing the diaper bag onto my shoulder and unhinge Jasmine's car seat. "Zach, I'll be done in about an hour," I tell the driver.

"Not a problem. I'll be here," he says with a smile.

The yoga studio wasn't an unknown place for me, but the class I had decided to take was. In the same vein, the yoga pants and sports bra under my coat were my normal accessories, but the baby I was bringing in with me was a decidedly new addition to the class.

I need to do something to relax, to decompress, and especially to let my loss of The Artemis Room go away, I had searched up some classes at a yoga studio I used to visit with Emma, but when checking out the schedule I noticed a Mommy and Me class that was supposed to strengthen the body after childbirth and help parents bond more strongly with their infants. Seemed like a win-win, so I signed up.

Being my first class, I chose the lighter baby and brought Jasmine, leaving her heftier brother back home with Lily. Jasmine, while louder, is also a bit calmer and less likely to try and jump out of my arms at any moment.

The studio is a little red brick building, unassuming and uncrowded, but inside it's ridiculously peaceful, full of soft music, piles of pillows in place of chairs, and happy, relaxed employees.

"Welcome," a young man, his long blond hair gathered into a bun, says. "I'm assuming you two lovely ladies are here for the Mommy yoga class?"

I nod and he leads the way to one of the large open rooms that classes are held. There are other mothers here, with babies ranging from newborns to what looks to be kids nearly one year old. Everyone is happy and chatting, some of the older babies sitting with each other and playing while the younger ones rest in their mother's arms, eyes wide and watching.

It feels weirdly like high school, as if I'm the new girl in class, but I straighten my shoulders, hanging my coat up on the rack and unstrapping Jasmine from her carrier. She's warm and isn't too pleased to be removed from her comfortable sanctuary, but her verbal complaints die out as soon as she's able to get a good look around.

It's an intimate room, with string lights and colorful lanterns hanging everywhere. The floors are covered with a padded mat, and I find an empty spot towards the back of the room, rolling out the yoga mat I had plucked from the diaper bag.

"You ready to do some serious workouts, kid?" I ask Jasmine, who blinks owlishly back at me but doesn't answer.

"First time?" a voice asks from next to me.

I smile shyly and nod. "Yeah. I haven't really exercised since birth. You think this is a good first class to get back in the swing of things?"

The woman, who seems to be in her late twenties with a distinctly Scandinavian look to her, hefts her son on her hip. "It's great. If I hadn't found this class, I may have never started exercising again. I'm Helga, and this little one is Freddie." She gives me a friendly grin, obviously waiting for my name back.

"Petra," I say simply before fluffing my daughter's hair. "And this is Jasmine."

"Well, if she's anything like my Fred, then this will be the highlight of her week. I think it's because Fred knows it makes me exhausted, so I'm more likely to let him watch television."

I laugh, but before I can ask anything else about the class, the instructor comes in. Instead of a baby, she's holding a vaguely annoyed tan French bulldog under one arm. The instructor is petite, but I can see the muscles shift under her skin when she moves.

"Namaste, everyone. I'm Kiki, and this is Alfredo." She holds the dog up for the class, and moms and children both make adoring noises. "If you're new to the class, yes, he's a dog. But I can't be popping out a new kid every year for this class, now can I?"

I look over at Helga, who shrugs. "She's not wrong."

Well, alright. Let's see how this thing goes, dog or no dog.

Kiki leads us through the opening poses, and Jasmine seems unsure about the entire ordeal initially, but when I lunge into warrior pose one, a hand supporting her bottom and the other wrapped around her middle, I hear her give a tentative chuckle.

I'm thrilled she's enjoying herself, but man, even my diminutive five-month-old is getting a little heavy. Most kids Jasmine's age weigh around sixteen pounds, while Jas clocks in at around twelve. But wow... Twelve pounds seems pretty heavy about fifteen minutes into this session!

"You are incredible, you are strong," Kiki intones to the class. "You carried these children in your bodies for months upon months, and now you carry them outside, rebuilding your bodies with the help of your little ones. Now breathe..."

The class is only thirty minutes long and as quivery as my arms are, I'm starting to realize something. Looking at my body in the mirror this morning, or anytime, doesn't really show me my body at all. It's something like this, working myself into a sweat, or something like surviving my high-risk pregnancy, that gives me the actual picture of how strong my body really is.

We finish in Goddess pose, and I'm holding Jasmine like a wiggly talisman in front of me. She coos, grabbing my fingers with her chubby hands. I look down at her, and even though she feels like the heaviest object in the universe to me right now, I am filled with warm affection. Affection and awe. Jasmine, whether she knows it or not in this moment, is just as much a warrior as I am. We both survived the pregnancy, and now, we both thrive, here in this yoga studio surrounded by all the other warrior mothers.

The scar did matter, but only as a reminder of all we had been through, and for once, I could see why Alex found it so beautiful.

* * *

On my way back home, I feel not only calmer and more serene but also filled with an incredible boost of self-confidence and energy. This class was truly amazing in so many different ways. Heck, I even feel like I could climb a mountain in one breath. Okay, maybe not a mountain, but instead of giving up on The Artemis Room, why don't I try calling the new owners of the place and buying it directly from them? I'm sure if I offer them double, they'll accept it.

Being decided and quite optimistic with my plan, I make a quick Google search until I land on a website that gives me the landlord details of any building in New York City. As I type in The Artemis Room's exact address, I land on Nico Tucci's details. Well, crap, the database hasn't been updated yet with the new owners.

I try another website, and then another, but all of them lead back to Nico.

I could wait a few more days for the details to be updated, or I could try directly asking my lawyer to see if she could check the public records on my behalf. Given the fact I'm pretty impatient, I take my phone and call Anna Griffith.

"Yes?" I hear from the other side of the line.

"Hi, Anna, this is Petra," I begin.

"Oh, Petra, so good to hear from you again. How have you been?" she asks with a very pleasant voice.

"Um, I'm doing well, thank you." After the formalities and small talk, I jump right into the subject. "Is it possible to get the contact info of the new owners of the building where

The Artemis Room used to be located? They purchased the place like yesterday."

"Oh, only yesterday?" she repeats in surprise. "That's gonna be hard as most databases won't have been updated yet." *Well, yeah, that I know...* "But I'm gonna do my best to find out. I'll call you back in a few minutes, alright?"

"Thank you so much," I tell her. "I look forward to hearing your findings."

I hang up, my heart filled with hope. If I can make it work, it will be a miracle. That place was made for me. It was made for art, not for a freaking restaurant. I take this moment to check on Jasmine, who is quietly sleeping beside me in her car seat—a reminder of another miracle that occurred not too long ago. The drive back home is quiet. Zach had turned off the radio, so I put on my headphones and start listening to some music and looking outside of my window to the city passing in front of me, but truly I'm already daydreaming again about my new gallery.

Twenty minutes later, as Zach announces our arrival home, he parks into the underground garage and turns off the engine. My phone starts ringing again, as if on cue, with my lawyer's name flashing on the screen. Oh gosh! My heart is already bouncing hard in my chest in anticipation and without any further ado, I take her call immediately.

"Hey," Anna starts. "So I found out the new details but there's only the name of their property management firm. Do you still want the contact of the manager?"

"Oh," I utter, quite intrigued at the finding. "Yes, that's okay, I'll contact them myself a bit later."

"Very well. I'm sending you their details to your mobile number."

"Thank you," I tell her. "I truly appreciate it."

"It's my pleasure," she answers. "Good luck."

After ending the call, I go to my message app and find the contact details of a certain Derek Fletcher, one of the property managers at a company called *B&L Management*. Decided, I dial his phone number and put the phone against my ear. The ringtone goes on, and on, and on...

A male voice from the other side answers in a hurry, "Yes?"

"Hello, is this Derek Fletcher from B&L Management and the property manager of the building where The Artemis Room was previously located?" I ask, just to confirm I'm talking to the right person.

"Yes, I am," Derek replies. "How may I help you?"

"Well, I'd like to buy that building and I'm ready to make an offer to your client."

"The building was just sold yesterday," he answers. "And I don't think they are interested in selling it any time soon."

"Not even for double what they bought it for?" I keep asking.

"No, not even for double," Derek replies, sounding quite sure of himself. "Our client wanted that building in particular."

"Can you at least ask them?" I insist, unconvinced. "Tell them I'm open to negotiate."

Derek exhales loudly from the other side, most likely displeased at my request. "Fine, I will, but I'm afraid you're just setting yourself up for disappointment, Miss," he says in a rush, which makes me believe he's just telling me that for the sake of ending the phone call. "Is there anything else I can help you with?

"Please do your very best to at least get them to listen to my offer."

Derek doesn't answer immediately. Maybe it's the tone in my voice that has made him reconsider my request. After a few beats of silence, he finally says, "Alright, I will do my best. What's your name again?"

"Um, Petra Van Gatt," I reply, realizing I didn't even introduce myself at the beginning.

"Duly noted. I'll try my best. Have a good day, then." And the manager just hangs up.

Well, I don't think he'll be calling me back anytime soon. I sounded insistent, desperate, and truly pathetic. Geez, of course, they aren't interested. If they really wanted that building in particular for whatever reason, I have zero chance of getting it back. I sigh, my heart pulling out of my chest at the loss of my dear Artemis Room.

I truly have to forget that building once and for all. Obsessing over it is not doing me any good.

CHAPTER 6

Manhattan, November 25, 2021
Petra

"May I?" Alex asks, after knocking a few times on the bedroom door. For some reason, each time he knows the babies, Lily, and I are in there, he always knocks softly before entering our bedroom.

"Sure," I reply as my eyes grace him.

My husband looks like his normal handsome self with a suit jacket and button-down, but he's relaxed enough to pair it with jeans and brown leather Chelsea boots. The kids and I on the other hand... well. It *is* a holiday, so I'm allowed to be a little extra.

During my Macy's trip, I picked up a few more items, including holiday outfits for the twins and me. My dress is a dark evergreen, hugging the curves of my body before flaring out at the waist and ending at the knees. It has long sleeves and a wide neckline, displaying a large amount of pale skin. I have complemented it with a simple pearl necklace, black flats, and dark pantyhose. I stare at my own reflection for a full five minutes, brushing my carefully curled hair back off my shoulders and touching up the smoky eye makeup. I feel... like myself.

I feel beautiful.

Jasmine and Jasper also look spectacular if I do say so myself. They're both wearing white shirts emblazoned with dozens of pumpkins, topped with brown corduroy overalls. Jasper's outfit ends in pants that look normal from the front, but they have a bright, multi-feathered turkey tail on the butt. Jasmine has a fluffy tulle skirt in a variety of reds and oranges, brown tights, and my very favorite addition... a huge orange and white headband bow on her little round head.

"Isn't Jasmine lovely with this headband?" Lily asks him, gushing over the bow just as I had.

But Alex who now stands beside us just sighs when he sees it. "She doesn't even have hair yet."

"She does, yes!" I insist, brushing my fingers across her wisps of brown fuzzy hair. "And she looks beautiful."

"I never said she didn't," Alex counters. "I just said that the bow is stupid."

"*You* are stupid," I shoot back, and Alex guffaws, holding his hands up in front of him.

"Okay, okay, you win." Alex takes Jasmine into his arms and gives her a big smooch on her little head.

I roll my eyes, ignoring his teasing. I think I've grabbed everything we will need for today, but if parenting has taught me anything, it's that something will always be forgotten. Oh well, we'll survive.

Leaving the house is an ordeal. Alex is driving today, and we have to pack both Pack 'n Plays along with the diaper bags before we can take the twins out.

Despite giving Lily the day off, she still wants to come with us to the underground parking to give us a hand.

"Are you sure you don't need me to join you?" she asks, concern written on her lovely face.

"I assure you, we've got these two munchkins under control," Alex responds, wiggling his fingers in front of Jasmine's face until she gives him a gummy smile.

"Yeah Lily, please go enjoy your child-free Thanksgiving. We'll see you tomorrow," I reassure her.

She heaves a sigh. "Okay, okay, I'm headed out then," she tells us, before taking me into her arms for a hug. "Call me if you need anything at all."

"We will," I answer back as Lily walks away. I slide a glance at Alex, a smirk playing on my lips. "She's nervous."

"Aren't you?" he asks, checking the buckles and straps on both babies' car seats, which are, of course, painfully frustrating to put in. How could they still be so difficult after all these years? Haven't companies invented anything better yet?

"No! Why would I be? We've taken them out a few times now."

"True, but we're in for a full day. Emma and Matt are one thing, but Roy and everyone else are bound to show up? You don't think they're going to get overstimulated?" Alex asks me, a tinge of worry in his voice.

Huh, I had no idea that he was bothered by our big Thanksgiving Day plans. "We'll be fine. I'm sure there'll be plenty of places at Dad's that we can stow them away for a quick sleep if we need to."

Alex mumbles under his breath, but I ignore him. His anxieties can't ruin how much I am looking forward to today. Why? Because Dad had bought a brand-new property, not too far from Emma's, and has decided to do the official inauguration today. According to him, it'd be his weekend residence. And just like the one we have in Bedford Hills, it's surrounded by nature, the Hudson River, and green scenery. For someone who loves Manhattan so much, I'm positively surprised that he has finally decided to spend some time away from the concrete jungle.

The drive to northern New York is uneventful, besides the expected influx of holiday traffic. Once we emerge from the city onto the open road a thick morning fog is hanging over the fields and valleys, casting everything in a gray and somber tone. The twins fuss for a bit initially, but the subtle vibrations of the car on the asphalt lull them into a peaceful sleep. Watching the trees and horizon pass, coupled with the silence, makes me sleepy too, and it's a conscious effort to delicately pillow my head on my hands against the window so I don't smudge my makeup.

"Have you been sleeping alright recently?" Alex rumbles from the driver's seat, having noticed my closed eyes.

"Mm-hm. Just been a busy few weeks."

It wasn't a lie either. Scheduling my classes for the next semester, taking the kids to their checkups, learning to juggle their ever-increasing needs throughout the day, trying to find another space for my gallery, and rebalancing myself months after the birth has taken so much of my energy. Anytime I could grab a quick snooze, I was all about it.

"Understood," Alex replies. He's quiet for a few minutes before clearing his throat. "How have you been feeling, though? You know... mentally?"

My eyes pop open, and I sit up with a sigh, rubbing my temples. So much for a quick nap.

Even though my depression is now over, this is something that stuck with him, and even months later Alex continues to check with me on the off chance I start to feel unlike myself again.

"I'm great, Alex. Promise. Just sleepy." I reach over and thread my fingers through his, and he gives me a relieved smile.

"Just checking. You know I have to look out for my little Petra." He pulls our clasped hands to his lips and brushes a kiss across my knuckles before releasing me.

I lean my head back on the window, considering. Truthfully, I had thought about continuing therapy even after my postpartum issues had been resolved. It had been liberating to speak everything on my mind, down to the last minuscule detail. Really, I was still considering it, but first I need to balance my schedule and make time throughout the chaos of the week. I am also not the best at forming routines.

The rest of the drive is quiet. Alex keeps the radio low to not awaken the sleeping beauties in the back seat, and when we finally make our way onto the driveway of my dad's new property, surrounded by perfectly manicured green lawns, I find I'm reluctant to wake them up to bring them in.

"They're going to be so cranky," I comment.

"Well, then, we'll dump them on Roy and go hide somewhere. He'll love it," Alex responds with a conspiratorial tone.

"You're joking, but he probably *would* love it. I have the feeling that he bought this place, especially for them."

Alex nods in agreement. "No doubt. He's softer than I've ever seen him. Sometimes I wonder if he's even the same man."

Dad has always been a man of few words and even fewer acts of affection. It wasn't until very recently with my mom's death and the pregnancy that his hard exterior started to melt. It will take a long time for me to open up to him entirely, but he is still my dad. Despite all our current issues, I love him endlessly. If he can change, I will be all the happier for it.

Actually, I hadn't truly believed his efforts were genuine until after the twins were born. With them, he has shown all the paternal love and affection I had craved as a child. He is warm and caring, always careful with them. And yet, when it comes to me, he still manages to get annoyed because I skipped a semester at Columbia. It's just unbelievable…

According to Alex, this new jovial Roy doesn't extend to him either. In fact, he is apparently even more of a hard ass at the office these days. The change is only for the babies, it seems.

Alex pulls smoothly into the circular driveway and parks in front of the house beside the other cars.

"Damn," I say as I look out of the window to the grand marble stairs and the balustrade leading to the front doors. Alex and I exit the car, and while he's already checking on little Jasper, I'm still taking in my surroundings. There is a small fountain in the center of the roundabout, the gardens surrounding us are lush and beautifully embellished with trees and flowers. The property itself looks exactly like a French chateau, and I wonder why on earth Dad needed to get such a big place all for himself.

I unhinge Jasmine's car seat as carefully as I can and holding her carrier, I make my way to the stairs alongside Alex and Jasper.

Once we reach the black iron doors, without bothering to knock, Janine greets us immediately.

"Welcome home!" she says, patting both my cheeks before bending over to peek in at sleeping Jasmine. "And welcome to you too, little miss."

"Don't forget I have two of them," I tell her with a laugh.

Janine looks affronted, placing her hands on her ample hips. "As if I'd forget the next troublemaker of the family." She makes the same motion as before, silently pulling the blanket covering Jasper's carrier aside to see his slumbering face. "They are growing so fast, my goodness."

She takes Jasper's carrier from Alex so he can bring in the rest of the baby gear from the car and waves me inside. As I step into the grand foyer, my eyes land on the marble stairs that stand before me, then they go to the sculptures and plants filling my surroundings, and then to the chandelier glittering from the high ceiling above me. The interior design is classic, matching perfectly well with its exterior.

"It's beautiful, isn't it?" Janine asks, leaning slightly closer to me. "Now let me show you the grand salon."

I follow her into what seems to be the living room where Dad and Matt are waiting, sipping port in front of a roaring fire.

I shoot Matt an amused look. "Are you even old enough to drink?"

They stop talking upon hearing me and they turn their attention to me. "If you can have babies, then I think I can have a drink," he shoots back, causing Dad to laugh.

"Enough squabbling, children," Dad interjects. "Put that baby down and come give your dad a hug."

Janine and I gently sit the carriers down by the sofa, and I check that both babies are both still slumbering peacefully before following Dad's directions and giving him a quick hug.

"Happy Thanksgiving, kid. Where is your husband? Slacking off as usual?"

"Hilarious," Alex says from the door, huffing as he plonks both unwieldy Pack 'n Plays down by the door. "You could have at least given me a hand, old man."

Both older men shake hands in greeting, slapping each other on the backs as if they hadn't just seen each other at work the other day. Matt greets Alex the same way, without the slap hug. I guess they aren't *quite* old friends yet.

"Dad, I invited Emma. I hope you don't mind," I comment, having a seat on the red leather sofa and holding my hands out to absorb the heat of the fire. "Her parents are having kind of a second honeymoon this year and she preferred to stay here."

"Not at all. We're going to be eating leftovers for years anyway; the more the merrier," he answers, pouring Alex a snifter of port.

Matt shifts uncomfortably. "Hey, uh, Roy? Did my dad ever respond to your invite?"

What? My dad invited Eric? After everything he did to our family? He must be kidding!

Dad sighs, rubbing the back of his neck. "Sorry, son. Eric never got back to me."

And I sigh too, but in relief. At least Eric has got some decency. It'd have been a horrible idea to have him here. Alex might have forgiven Matt, but he'll never forgive his dad for what he did to us.

Matt's shoulders slump, yet he doesn't look very surprised. "I figured as much. Thanks for trying."

Alex and I look at each other uncomfortably, not knowing what to say, but we are saved when Emma appears in the doorway, a bottle of wine bedecked with a gold bow clutched in her hand.

"Fuck that guy," Emma proclaims, walking in like she owns the place. Janine, who must have let her in, winces at the coarse language, taking the wine meant as a gift along with Emma's trademark leather jacket.

"What she said," Alex says to me under his breath, and I have to suppress a giggle.

But my giggle fades away as soon as my eyes fall on an older woman making her way in with Sarah, Matt's girlfriend.

"Oh, hey," Sarah says, looking at me, her tone always as bubbly. She gives me a quick hug, before shaking hands with everyone else.

While I can't figure out why Matt wanted to bring his Dad here, I can understand why he invited Sarah. After all, it's Thanksgiving and they've become quite serious over the past few months. But my attention is particularly perked at the older woman, sporting a classy haircut, blond straight hair brushing her shoulders, a discreet pair of diamond earrings, and an elegant fit-and-flare black lace dress falling below her knees.

"Petra," Dad says as he goes to stand beside her. They exchange a weird look and I start to wonder what the heck is going on between the pair. I notice how uncomfortable they have become, now that introductions have to be made. "This is Catherine Dubois, a very dear friend of mine."

My brows raise up immediately. A very *dear* friend? What the heck does that even mean? In my nineteen years of life, Dad has never introduced me to any woman that way. Is she just a friend or is she his friend with benefits, like Sarah was to Matt before they became official?

Oh jeez, my heartbeat rises at the idea of Dad having a serious girlfriend.

No, no, no, and no! That can't be possible! She would never be more than a friend, right?

I do my best to conceal my astonishment and make a conscious effort to smile politely and extend a hand to shake hers. "Hi, Ms. Dubois. Very nice to meet you." That's the best I can do at this point.

"Oh, please, call me Catherine," she says with a pleasant voice and French accent. Instead of taking my hand, she steps forward and gives me two cheek kisses. "It's wonderful to finally meet you in person. Roy has spoken so much about you that it feels like I've already known you for years."

"Oh, he did?" My gaze goes right to my dad, who clears his throat and looks away in embarrassment. "How did you two meet?" I ask Catherine, already impatient to know all the gritty details.

"What if we talk a bit more about it later on, huh?" Dad interjects as he starts ushering me out of the living room and back to the grand foyer. "It's your first time here, so let me show you around."

If he thinks giving me a tour of his house will make me forget my question he's very mistaken.

Before I can refuse though, Catherine takes over. "That's a great idea." *Why am I not surprised by her comment?* "I'll stay with the rest of the guests," she says, leaving us alone.

Without much of a choice left, I follow Dad and we take the marble stairs. We climb in silence, our footsteps being the only sound between us.

A million questions start buzzing around my mind, but one in particular is imploring to be answered. "What do you mean by a very *dear* friend?"

Dad chuckles in return, his gaze fixed in front as we reach the first floor. The hallway of the first floor matches the interior design of the foyer and it's just as spacious. He turns to his right and I follow him across the hall.

A few steps farther in, Dad hasn't said a word. His silence is killing me slowly.

"So?" I ask loud enough for him to hear.

"So…" he stops in front of a door and opens it. "This is the library of the house." He steps aside, inviting me in first. Maybe this tour was an excuse for us to go to a quieter place so that we could talk. Either way, I walk in and Dad closes the door behind him. The library is very similar to the one we have in Bedford Hills. There's an office desk, a big window behind it, walls filled with books, and a sitting area on my left. "As you can see, I even have first editions of many of your favorite books."

Dad is about to go and take a few books when I ask, "Who is she?" My tone is more insistent than before since Dad has been trying hard to avoid the subject.

He turns to face me, a small smile playing at the corner of his lips. "Well, she is a friend of course," he answers vaguely.

"She doesn't seem to be *just* a friend though."

He presses his lips together, his gaze drifting away for a moment. "She's a bit more than that," he finally confesses.

My heart sinks at his answer. Oh *goodness*…"Is she your girlfriend?" Even the word *girlfriend* tastes bittersweet when it comes to my dad.

"I wouldn't go as far as saying that, but we have been getting along…"

"Getting along?" I repeat in confusion. A sigh rolls off my mouth, tired of his nonsense. "Are you guys together, yes or no?"

He cocks his head to the side, pondering his next set of words. "It's complicated…"

"Only if you want it to be."

"Alright, alright," he presses, before exhaling loudly in return. Then a few beats of silence ensue, but Dad finally proceeds, "Catherine and I have a wonderful relationship. I don't know what I'd call it exactly, but it's great. She's a, um, a great *compagne*." *Compagne* is the French equivalent of either partner, companion, or even girlfriend! Is he using the French language to remain as vague as he can?

I walk towards him and holding him by the arms, I search for his gaze, forcing him to face me. "Do you know her well? Are you sure she isn't with you just because of your wealth?"

"Argh…" he rolls his eyes in annoyance and takes a few steps away. "No, Catherine is from the French nobility. She comes from old money. She was born and raised in it."

"How did the two of you meet?" I ask him since he's finally opening up.

Dad heaves a sigh, considering my question. "We met in the Netherlands, a long time ago."

"I want specifics."

Despite knowing he's getting annoyed at my demands, he says, "We were introduced to each other by some mutual friends." And for the sake of ending the subject, he adds, "She is trustworthy, don't worry."

But I've got more to ask. "Was she married before?"

"Oh, c'mon," Dad snaps. "Why so many questions?"

"Because I'm curious," I answer with an innocent tone.

"She has been married once before. Just like me." I can see the trace of a smile settling on his lips as he thinks something through. "We have a lot in common, actually."

I nod pensively, before looking him in the eye and saying, "Keep your head on your shoulders, alright?"

"Me?" He looks at me with astonishment. "I'm not the one who skipped out a whole semester at Columbia."

Geez! His comment hits me unexpectedly and I scoff at him. "I can't believe you're still mad at me because of that."

"I'm not mad, just…" he looks down, searching for the best words to put on, "disappointed in your decision."

"In a month and a half I'm gonna resume classes," I tell him, my heart taking a reel at his obtuse attitude. It hurts seeing how insensitive he can be regarding my situation. "I went through an incredibly invasive surgery that took weeks to heal, then I had to deal with postpartum depression—"

"Maybe if you had resumed classes earlier, you wouldn't have been depressed," he interposes, his tone rising. My eyes widen in shock and I'm totally taken aback by his statement. Wow. What a fucking asshole he can be. A cold silence settles between us for a moment before Dad proceeds. "The twins were in the NICU for weeks. I don't get why you had to spend the entire time sitting there doing nothing." I shake my head, looking at him in disgust. Now I understand why he didn't want to answer my calls; if he were about to tell me all these cruel words over the phone, I would've never bothered to show up today.

"Wow," I utter, not knowing what else to say. He actually managed to leave me speechless. I want to cry from how much his words have hurt me, but I make a conscious effort to sniffle back my tears and take some deep breaths in and out. As I get calmer, I steady myself and tell him a few truths he needs to know. "Well, because they are my children and I had no idea if they would pull through or not." My voice is not loud or even emotional, it's actually pretty contained, but it's also tired—of his bullshit. "Just because you don't understand my reasoning, doesn't mean it's not valid."

Dad shuts his eyes and presses his eyelids as the tension between us remains barely tolerable. "That's not what I meant," he says under his breath, reopening his eyes. "But if you'd resumed college earlier, you'd have been less anxious about their state at the NICU," he adds. "That's all."

I shake my head in disagreement, and my stare goes toward the window where the sunlight is emanating. I focus my attention there, but a sigh rolls off my mouth as I think how ridiculous his attitude is.

"Look, what is done is done." My stare follows his voice and I find Dad walking in my direction, most likely trying to build a bridge between us after the chaotic discussion we just had. His face holds some candid sadness, and dare I say, some remorse? Standing in front of me, he holds my shoulders, his eyes pinned on mine. "Today is thanksgiving. We are not going to be mad at each other, are we?"

"Well, you're the one who started it," I refute.

"Because you were insinuating I could lose my mind for a woman."

"A lot of men do."

Dad shakes his head, a small smile playing at the corner of his lips. "I'm too old for that."

There is no age to fall in love. But I refrain from telling him that.

"Well, shall we see the rest?" he asks, which is also a way for him to put our discussion behind us.

I flash him a half-smile. "Alright, let's see your new baby."

* * *

After the house tour finishes, we go back to the living room to join the rest of the guests. We spend the afternoon in companionable conversation, gathered in front of the bright fireplace as we wait for dinner to get ready. While everyone seems to be engrossed in the current story Dad is recounting, I can't stop wondering who this Catherine Dubois that stands beside him is, and why he seems to be admiring her so much. She looks younger than Mom, but not by too much. Wrinkles have already perked around her eyes despite the perfect makeup. She's however very classy and elegant. Dad has good taste, that I have to admit. As soon as Catherine starts speaking, I notice how his face brightens up with a big smile and his eyes glitter like two bright diamonds.

"I'm glad you bought this place," she tells him with a honey voice like we aren't even here. "You needed a quieter place to relax and escape the craziness of that city. You've been way too stressed lately."

Lately? How well does she know him to say something like that? And how long has she been around? Damn. I should've asked more questions about her when we were in his office, but he seemed so annoyed already.

"*I'm too old for this,*" I recall him saying.

Yeah, right...

Eventually, Janine walks in to join us while she waits on the turkey to finish cooking. I had offered to bring my own entrée, but she had insisted that the turkey itself was the only thing that wasn't vegan being served. All the sides and desserts were safe, and Dad had even gone as far as to order a few servings of Thanksgiving tofurkey from a local vegan restaurant.

Dad starts enquiring about the poor turkey in the oven and Janine becomes the center of attention. I take this opportunity to look at Emma and with a head nod, I instruct her to follow me out of the living room, and we head to a quiet place right behind the marble stairs.

There, I give a quick glance around us and seeing we are totally alone, I lower my voice and ask, "Did you know about her?"

"Of course not," she snaps instantly, matching my barely audible tone. "Did your dad tell you who she is?"

"Very little; just that she's from a French noble family," I disclose, giving another glance above Emma's shoulder. "But he's acting very weird every time I try to get to know more about her."

Emma nods, considering me. "Yeah, and the way he looks at her…"

"Oh gosh, don't even talk about it," I interpose immediately, cringing as I picture exactly that. "She speaks like they've known each other for years."

"Like they have been *together* for years," she corrects, making my heart squeeze tight at the idea.

"It can't be," I reply. "Why would he have taken so long to introduce us to her?"

"I don't know." Emma shrugs, and we keep quiet for a moment as I remain thinking about this mysterious woman. And just as if Emma had read my mind, she asks, "Look, um, do you want me to do a background check on her?"

A quick smile escapes me—this is exactly what I needed. "If you don't mind…"

"Of course I don't." She gives me a quick pat on the arm, before adding, "It might take a while before I get a complete dossier about her, but by next month I should have some breaking news."

"Thank you, Emma," I answer, my heart filled with gratitude. "By next month is fine." After all, December is in just five days.

"Well, let's go back inside before they start wondering what we are up to."

Once we return to the living room, Emma serves herself a new glass of port and we sit beside each other on the couch where Alex is already enjoying another glass of wine. Meanwhile, Janine brings me a warm glass of rum apple cider as if she felt that I also needed a drink. I would've declined alcohol in normal circumstances, but today I truly need a beverage that would relax me. After all, the idea that my dad could have been with that woman for years while I knew nothing about it isn't sitting well with me.

When my little Jasmine wakes up, Janine insists on holding her so that I can finish my drink. Jasper follows suit and we hear him babbling and blowing raspberries in his carrier. I stand to retrieve him, but Dad waves me off.

"Let me get my grandson. You just sit and enjoy the parade!" he says, groaning as he kneels to unbuckle Jasper.

"The parade?" I ask in confusion, looking at my husband for answers. But eventually, I understand he was talking about the pre-recorded parade, playing on the TV.

Wait—what? Dad even turned on the TV? Wow.

"Roy, I don't even know who you are anymore," Alex comments, reading exactly my mind as he swirls his port in his snifter.

"A grandpa, that's who," Dad responds, hugging his squirming grandson close before sitting down with him on his lap.

Yeah, a pity he wasn't as sweet and lovely with me earlier today.

It turns out the twins are huge fans of the Macy's Thanksgiving Day Parade on television, watching with their mouths open and their eyes wide. They'd never watched TV before, so it must be a one-of-a-kind experience for them. All the colorful floats and musical productions hold their attention completely. Maybe next year we would take them to see it in person, as long as we could procure a spot somewhere safely away from the crowds.

The Westminster Dog Show that comes on after the parade is a close second for favorite shows, especially with Jasper, who claps and squeals with each close up of a dog that appears on screen. Jasmine is mildly interested but is wiggling in Janine's grip soon enough, and the latter insists on feeding her when I get up to do so. I plop back down on the couch, shrugging at Alex. I guess neither of us is touching our children today.

I'm feeling already flushed from the rum cider burning in my empty stomach, so when Janine, with Jasmine on her hip, declares dinner is ready, I'm more than ready to eat. It's Thanksgiving, so of course dinner is being served at five in the evening instead of traditional dinner time. The plan had been for the twins to chill in their playpens while we eat, but Dad surprises us by busting out two high chairs.

"He's got a whole room of unopened baby things in the basement," Janine whispers to me covertly. "I guess he wanted to make sure they wouldn't miss anything while being here."

Surprised, I watch my Dad and Alex set the chairs up at the dining table. Did he really go that far for the twins? I swear to myself that I'll bring them over to visit more after seeing the get-up. He is clearly expecting to see them often.

Since Eric didn't show, Janine joins us for dinner. The atmosphere is comforting and homey, the air full of the sound of clinking silverware and the smells of a decadent homemade meal. Everything is delicious, and we even chance feeding a few tiny tastes of mashed sweet potatoes to the twins. They appear shocked at the flavor explosion, smacking their lips. Matt raves about his YouTube channel, to the amusement of no one, but we all nod along until he tires himself out and Sarah gives him a peck on the cheek. A small smile stretches up at my lips as I see the gesture—they look really sweet together. Dad quickly picks up the conversation before Matt can think of anything else to go on about.

"So Petra, Alex said you were in the market for a place to start your own gallery?"

The question makes me tense. Why on earth did Alex tell him about my situation? I let out a long sigh, playing with the base of my glass as I think about it. "Yeah, I shouldn't be, but here I am…"

"Why not?" he asks, most likely knowing already the answer. "Is it because you wanted the building that used to house that gallery you liked so much?"

My chest tightens a little at the mention of The Artemis Room. The sale of my beloved gallery still stings, and in the few days after my call with the new property manager I had made sure to have Zach take the long way around so I didn't have to see the new owners moving trucks pouring into the place.

Two days ago we had to pass the gallery on the way to the pediatrician, and there were blessedly no signs of the eventual restaurant yet, but the empty walls I saw when I briefly glanced through the open windows broke my heart a little. The building looked hollow and sad after decades of being full of vibrant art. It should never, ever have to look that way.

I take a deep breath and plaster on a fake smile. "Yeah, it's unfortunate, but it was sold to a hospitality brand. I hope that the new owners take care of the place like it deserves."

Dad nods in understanding. "Look, after a while, disappointments like that won't bother you so much, and if life has taught me anything, it's that second chances come around when you least expect them."

"Sure, Dad," I respond vaguely, ready to change the subject. I feel Alex squeeze my knee in solidarity beneath the table before he asks Dad something about Gatt-Dieren Capital and the two men launch into work talk.

I look in front of me at the woman sitting beside my dad. Ms. Dubois has been quiet for most of the dinner. Pressing my lips together, I ponder whether or not I should start a conversation with her, but for better or worse, I ask the very same question I had to her earlier in the day. "So Catherine, how did you and my dad meet exactly?"

Emma's attention perks up immediately, and she puts her cutlery down.

Catherine gives me a small smile, cleans her mouth with her white napkin, and ponders my question for a second. "We met in the Netherlands," she begins. "I was freshly divorced, and I went to an event your dad was also attending. We had some mutual friends, and they introduced us."

"What kind of event?" Emma asks before I can do so.

"Just a business event, actually," she answers.

"You work?" The question rolls off my tongue instantly, without me stopping to think.

"Petra, c'mon, why are you bothering Catherine with so many questions?" Obviously, Dad is already coming to her rescue.

"It's okay, Roy." She gives him a quick pat on the hand before her attention returns to me. "It was an event for family offices, so yes, I was present."

"Oh, I see…" I mumble. Despite wanting to push the conversation further, I refrain from doing so knowing that Dad would rebuke me again if I tried. And I'm definitely not interested in creating more friction between us, especially not on Thanksgiving. Yet I can't help wondering why he is so worried about me asking questions relating to her? Is he afraid I'm not gonna like her? Or is he afraid that I will find the truth about his relationship with her? Oh gosh, what if Emma was right, and they have been together for a long time? One thing is sure: whatever he is trying to hide, sooner or later, I'll find out.

Dinner winds down, finished off with pumpkin pie, as is tradition. Janine and I feed the twins their bottles, and I give them each a spoon of whipped cream, which they seem to enjoy even more than the sweet potatoes. Soon enough, they would be eating dinner with Alex and me, and all my worries about feeding Jasmine solids will be long behind us. Damn. My little ones are growing so quickly!

Full of milk and special Thanksgiving treats, the twins are more than ready for a nap. We set the Pack 'n Plays up in the small study that adjoins the living room, gently laying them down to rest, before joining everyone else for after-dinner drinks.

The lights are low in the living room now, and conversations are quieter. We're all completely stuffed, and in the long moments of silence here and there, I can hear the comforting crackling of the logs in the fireplace.

Eventually, close to nine pm, the twins start to fuss in the other room. "That's our cue to head out," Alex says, standing up to stretch. "We need to get the twins their bath."

The whole group tag teams carrying our plethora of baby supplies out to the car, and when I emerge into the open air, Jasmine held in my arms, the chill of winter is readily apparent. I look up into the darkening sky just as fat, fluffy snowflakes begin to fall, and one lands right on Jasmine's button nose. She grimaces from the cold, wiping at her face, but the tiny moment warms my soul.

No matter what happened between my dad and me, it has been such a wonderful day.

CHAPTER 7

Manhattan, November 30, 2021
Petra

I woke up early this morning, the urge to paint having dug into me during my sleep. I had been dreaming of a new art collection inspired by the transition of seasons that happens in nature but also in us. I am not one for alarms, preferring to sleep as much as possible, but I know good and well that these upcoming weeks are going to be chaotic with the amount of Christmas events and dinners Alex and I have to attend. All I want to do for now is put my brush to the canvas and heal once and for all from the pain of losing my dear Artemis Room to that hospitality brand. It has been two weeks since Nico sent me that dreadful message, but it's still something I haven't managed to let go of completely.

Today Alex is able to work from home, so I decide to bring him a coffee with a good morning kiss. He looks at me quite surprised by my unexpected visit but he seems to love it anyway. Then I head to the nursery to greet the twins and Lily, who's already busy getting them ready for the day.

They are extra rambunctious, and they have no reservations about letting us know it.

"Ba ba. BA BA BA," Jasmine chants, demanding our full, undivided attention. Lily and I look at each other, sharing a smile up to our ears, yet unsure if the little girl is just stringing sounds together, or if she actually knows what she's referencing, but nonetheless we listen to the missy in awe and bring her the breakfast bottle.

Jasper is more reserved in the early talking department, settling for low whispers of, "Ma, ma, ma ma," as he plays, his little brows drawn together in concentration. He's turning out to be quite the little tinkerer, taking great enjoyment in toys that come apart. He hasn't mastered reassembling, but it's a start.

"What's on your agenda today?" Lily asks me, looking radiant in a cerulean blue skirt and ivory blouse.

"I need to get some painting done. Alex is home today, so if you need an extra hand, would you mind going to him today instead?"

"Absolutely. The best mothers are the ones that take time for themselves and their passions, too," Lily responds encouragingly.

I give both babies kisses on their plump cheeks, nuzzling them close and breathing in their baby smell. I could spend all day in here, no matter how exhausting the twins may be, and never get sick of it, but Lily is right. I have been neglecting my own interests and hobbies, and that just isn't healthy for anyone.

I leave the nursery, closing the door quietly behind me, hoping that the twins don't notice my departure, and head to the stairs that will take me to one of my favorite places in the world: my atelier.

I haven't been there in ages and my heart pants in excitement at the idea of painting again. As I enter, I can't help but smile at the floor-to-ceiling windows that bathe the room in buttery sunlight. The walls and ceilings are painted in varying shades of white, eggshell, and beige. No distracting or clashing colors.

Most of the time, the atelier reflects the chaos of my creative mind. Finished projects leaning up against the walls with half-completed canvases. I reach for my smock hanging on the hook behind the door and tie it around my waist. The familiar motion helps to switch my brain from "mom mode" back to "regular Petra" and I take in a deep breath, reveling in the smells of oil and turpentine. It smells like heaven.

I take a few steps into the room and stop in my tracks, looking around. For a second, I can't pinpoint what exactly is wrong, but after a few confused blinks my brain catches up with my eyes and I realize the problem: My paintings are all gone! Even the one that Alex had bought me by Pierre Soulages! And all of my paints are neatly arranged on one of my storage desks. The easels are folded up and stored against the wall, and all the blank canvases are arranged on the shelving. It's organized, empty, and so not me.

Where the heck could my paintings have gone? Nervousness fills me. What if Alex had hired a cleaning service, and they misunderstood, tossing my paintings out with the garbage on accident? My hand shakes minutely as I press the intercom button.

"Uh, Maria? Can you come to the atelier, please?"

The housekeeper arrives a few minutes later, looking worried. "Are you alright, ma'am? You sounded upset. I hurried up here as fast as I could."

I wring my smock in my hands. "Maria, do you know why my paintings are gone?"

She pokes her head into the atelier and frowns. "I don't know ma'am, I'm sorry. Mr. Van Dieren was up here a few times last week, but he told me not to worry about anything. Maybe he knows a bit more?"

"Alright, I'll go and ask him."

I descend the stairs with my heart in my throat, resisting the urge to barge into Alex's office without knocking. Despite anxiously wanting an answer, I make the conscious effort to knock for the sake of politeness and slowly, I push the door open, seeing Alex in what appears to be a Zoom meeting. I wince when he rotates his chair towards me, but he doesn't seem annoyed, holding up a finger to let me know he'll be right with me.

"Can you excuse me one moment?" he asks politely, before raising up from his seat.

He joins me in the hallway, looking over my paint-stained smock before his eyes land on my face, where he immediately reads my worry. "What's wrong, love?" he asks, brushing a strand of hair behind my ear.

"All my paintings are gone. Even the one from Mr. Soulages! I'm freaking out! Do you know where they could be?"

He immediately relaxes. "Ah, yeah, I apologize. I forgot to tell you. The interior designers painted your atelier with the wrong paint. It'll start to peel and flake after too much exposure to turpentine. I'm just having the room repainted with the right stuff, so I had your paintings moved to your old studio at Roy's, that's all."

My shoulders sag in relief and I stand on my tiptoes to kiss him before falling back. "Thank goodness, I shouldn't have worried. You always know exactly what's going on. Is it safe for me to paint there today, though?"

"Yes, of course. Whatever you finish, I'll have removed once it's dry. The painters are coming this weekend." Something pings on his smartwatch, and he checks it with a sigh. "I've got to get back to work. Just have Maria make a note of when your piece will be done, and I'll have it moved."

"Okay thanks, baby."

Alex returns to work, and I jog up the stairs back to the atelier. Now that Alex has eased my mind, I can get started.

Every little girl that ever wanted to be a painter dreamed of a studio like this, and it makes me giddy still to gather my chosen paints for the day. I pick out an array of reds, oranges, browns, and greens. Lily and I had taken the twins on a walk through Central Park in the strollers the other week on a particularly warm day, and though some of the trees had dumped their leaves to the ground, there were enough of them still wreathed in their fall colors to inspire me. Autumn was slowly but surely receding into winter and it's that natural transition from one season to another that I had wanted to paint ever since. It reminded me of us—humans, and the different seasons of life.

Yes! That's it!

The seasons of life will be the name of my new art collection! It's perfect.

I drag one of my biggest easels in front of the windows, placing the stool in front of it and dropping the paints on the lip of the easel. Next is a large canvas, 24 x 30, my mixing palette, and my brushes. I finish off my preparations with a large cup of water for brush washing and some soft rags. My back will face the windows, meaning I won't get to enjoy the beautiful view, but I will be able to paint in a wash of natural light; the best light for any artwork.

I ask the room's Alexa to play "painting playlist four," and the plucky sounds of an acoustic guitar float through the surrounding air. I hum along, knowing all of the songs by heart.

Painting is a part of me, something that is in my bones. Whenever I carry stress or burdens, I can bleed them out on the canvas, leaving me lighter than before. Or when my emotions are running high, the scrape of the brush against the white canvas is almost meditative, allowing me to get a hold of myself. I have been painting for as long as I can remember, and not to pat myself on the back too much, but I think I've made some good progress since Alex came to check my paintings out two years ago… Geez, time flies so fast.

As I come to think of it, even Alex's perfectionist of a snobby sister, Yara, had grudgingly admired my work, even conscripting me to paint a portrait of her. I shudder, remembering Yara's nude portrait. I'm really glad that today it'd be trees flowing from the tip of my brush and not the curves of Yara's body. Yuck…

The morning passes, the sun arching across the sky as I work. I lose myself in the paint. The music wraps around me, and time seems meaningless. There is only the mixing of colors, the stroke of the bristles, and the image in my mind pouring into reality. I'm transfixed, and I have to shake off the fog of it all when Maria brings up some finger foods for lunch. I thank her, loading a plate up with a few cucumber sandwiches and grabbing a glass of lemon water.

I had one overly plush chair up here for when I didn't want to fall out of the painting headspace but still needed a break. My comfy chair faces the windows, and I tuck my feet underneath me as I make myself comfortable, nibbling at my sandwiches.

It isn't a complicated piece. Everyone paints trees, and it's the perfect subject for someone that hasn't painted in a bit, but I still feel like something is missing. From experience, I know nothing will come to me if I dwell on the issue, so I focus on something else while I enjoy my lunch. Suddenly though, my phone buzzes, announcing a new SMS.

I take the phone from my pocket and slide up to read the new message from Emma: *"Any plans for your birthday? I was thinking to go away this weekend, but realized you're turning 20 on Sunday! X."*

Oh gosh, my birthday! My hand hits my forehead, embarrassed to have totally forgotten about it. Does Alex remember it's my birthday this Sunday? Should I remind him? And where are we having Christmas? We haven't even begun to discuss that yet. Geez, all I hope is that we won't have to go to his Mom's estate. I start on another tiny sandwich, considering the upcoming weeks. December is going to be incredibly busy. There's always a myriad of Christmas events to attend on behalf of Gatt-Dieren Capital that I would have to schedule my time pretty well if I wanted to sneak away and paint at all.

Hopefully, Alex's painters will have the atelier done in a day or two, so I won't have to abstain for too long. I know from experience that the less I paint, the less I want to paint, and when the urge finally strikes, I feel rusty and frustrated by the waning of my skills. I really need to keep on top of it.

I dust the crumbs off my hands, getting ready to get back to my painting when something catches my eye on the windowsill. Like a bright ruby, a male cardinal lands, joined immediately by a brown female, only the tips of her wings and the crest on her head scarlet. I keep still, watching as they stretch their wings wide and hop around the small outcropping of the building. The male is so incredibly red against the drab gray stone of the city that he looks like a drop of blood.

He's gorgeous. A little piece of wild nature visiting me here in Manhattan, along with his mate. They remain for maybe fifteen minutes before leaping back into the air, never leaving each other's side. Their visit had been brief, but they had given me a wonderful gift: inspiration.

I hop up from my seat and hurry back to the easel, cracking my knuckles and plucking my brush from the water, drying it on a towel. I know exactly what my painting is missing...

I fill in the trunks and the rest of the leaves of the trees, the blocks of color broken up by the thin tendrils of naked branches here and there. Once the trees are perfect, I add the final touch, given to me by the visit of my crimson friends. I paint a flock of cardinals, exploding from the trees into the air, tiny forms of red and brown. They add life to an otherwise lifeless scene, and once I put the finishing touches, I sit back from the painting, satisfied.

Not bad for someone that hasn't picked up a brush in months, I gloat internally.

The paint is still shiny and wet, so I resist the urge to continue tweaking the canvas and remove my smock. It'll need at least twenty-four hours to be fully dry. I find some satisfaction in my cleaning up rituals, capping my paints, and wiping any excess from the bottles and tubes, followed by washing my brushes in pungent turpentine and finally putting everything away in vaguely the right spot.

When I finish, it's almost six pm. I have been up here for hours without realizing it! But, I feel refreshed and especially accomplished to have started my new art collection. If I keep being just as focused I could do an extra four to five paintings before the end of the year. My head is clearer than it has been in weeks, and with such a goal in mind, I take this moment to text Emma back: *"I'm gonna stay home and paint. I'm working on a new art collection. Don't worry, we can meet another time. X,"* and I press *send.*

I guess Lily is right—good mothers make time for themselves.

CHAPTER 8

Manhattan, December 1, 2021
Petra

"That isn't looking too good there," Emma sermons me as I place the garland on top of the fireplace in the living room. While I truly appreciate her supposed good taste and perfectionist qualities, she has been such a piece of work during the entire condo's Christmas decorating project. Jesus Christ, I'd hate to think that she's also like that with her staff when they decorate the family estate. "Petra! Not there!" she screams again as I try different angles to fix the eucalyptus and white berry garland she picked out at Macy's for me. Displeased with my stubborn nature, she puts down her own box of Christmas accessories and hastens in my direction, taking the garland from my hands. She then goes to the low table and lays it flat on the center, styling a bit of the foliage for a finished look. A smile of pride and satisfaction slowly spreads across her lips, while I'm just left annoyed at the whole thing. "Here it looks good."

I heave a sigh, shaking my head. When she called this morning and asked if I wanted help with decorating the condo, I figured she wanted to come over and decorate it herself. After all, I'd never been into house decor, but I thought it could be fun to hang the Christmas decorations up with Emma since she likes these things so much. Boy, what a mistake! Next time, I'll just lock myself inside my atelier and keep painting while I let her do her thing.

"Not bad, huh?" Her voice pulls me away from my thoughts and we glance around the living room which is now filled with garlands, wreaths, fairy lights, one tall fir tree, Christmas statues perched on the walls, candles, and God knows what else might be hidden about. Honestly, the mix of white, green, red, golden, and silver tones blend perfectly well with the modern furniture, creating a cozy and wintery atmosphere.

"It looks great, yeah," I admit. "You're very talented when it comes to these things." As I come to think of it, I then add, "If you ever run out of money from your trust, you could make a living as an interior designer."

Emma snorts a bit at my comment as we both know this isn't gonna happen any time soon. "Thanks," she says for the sake of politeness, before giving a quick look at her watch. "Well, there's just the Christmas tree left to decorate, but I believe this is something you and Alex might want to do."

I give her a smile in return for the thoughtful gesture. Indeed, this is definitely something I'd like Alex and me to do together, and even get the kids to help a bit.

"Thank you for everything," I tell her as she walks back towards me. "Honestly, I wouldn't have done it without you."

Which is true. When I woke up this morning, decorating the condo for Christmas wasn't really something on my to-do list.

She gives me a warm pat in appreciation, and before she can say something else, we hear the front door unlocking and cracking open. I go and check who's here, and as I see Alex coming in, I take a quick glance at my watch only to realize it's already six p.m. Wow! Time truly flies when you have a whole condo to decorate.

My eyes meet his and, almost instinctively, I take a few more steps to stand before him, and raising up on my tiptoes, I clasp my arms around his neck and press my lips against his. I might have tasted his lips a thousand times, but they always manage to make me fly without leaving the ground. A few seconds later, Alex breaks our kiss, his curious gaze already lingering around the hallway at the fairy lights and garlands hanging from the ceiling.

"What do you think?" I ask, noticing the reflection of the fairy lights in his eyes as he keeps observing them. "There's just the tree missing to decorate, but I wanted to do it with you."

His gaze finally returns to meet mine, but he seems a bit confused. "That's really lovely, but, um, you want to stay here for Christmas?"

Now that's an odd question. "Well, you didn't say anything about traveling so I figured we'd be spending it here…"

Alex nods pensively before asking out of nowhere, "What if we were to go to Aspen instead? Just the four of us?"

"To Aspen?" I repeat, quite taken aback by his sudden suggestion. Geez, if Alex wanted to travel, then why on earth did I spend all day long decorating the condo? But my thoughts quickly switch to the wintery getaway and as I picture the four of us playing in the snow, my face instantly brightens with a huge smile. "That's a really good idea, actually! The kids are gonna love it!" And before Alex can add another word, I ask, "When are we leaving?"

Despite my excitement, he ponders for a few seconds before giving me an answer. "The last Christmas dinner we have to attend is on the twenty-first, so we can fly out the following morning."

I heave a sigh, knowing the next two weeks will be filled with overcrowded events that will do nothing but bore me to death. "Do we really have to attend all of them?" I bat my eyelashes with a pleasant smile trying to dissuade him, but Alex just snorts in return.

"Yes, Miss Petra, we do."

"Petra?" I hear Emma saying from behind me. I turn around and notice she's already wearing her coat again and holding her purse. "I'm gonna go since it's getting pretty late. If you guys need anything, just let me know."

Alex nods at her, while I go and bid her farewell.

"Thank you again for everything, Emma." I embrace her tightly into my arms and we remain standing there, reveling in each other's hug for a moment. After she releases me, she gives me a quick smile in appreciation and says, "Well, um, if you do anything for your birthday, let me know, okay?"

"I will," I reply, looking at her as she makes her way out. "Have a great evening."

Once the door clicks shut behind her, I take Alex's hand and lead him into the living room to show him what Emma and I—or mainly Emma—have done.

"Oh, wow," he utters, taking in his surroundings. "I never thought you liked decorating so much."

"Well, Emma did most of it… and trust me it was a whole ordeal." I look around, especially at the lit candles and green garlands. "It's beautiful though, isn't it?"

Alex nods. "Yeah, she did a pretty good job."

I'm about to invite him to decorate the Christmas tree when my phone suddenly starts ringing in the back pocket of my jeans. The sound is loud enough to make me stop in my tracks, and after a few more ringtones it's becoming impossible to just ignore it, so I grasp the phone and check who's calling me.

Oh, wow! Derek Fletcher from B&L Management? What a surprise! Why is he calling me now though? It has been what—ten days since I called him?

I turn around, ready to take the call somewhere else. "I'll be right back," I say before I exit the room, and go to the office of the house, shutting the door behind me. There, I press the green button and put the screen against my ear, excitement fluttering in my stomach in the hope he can bring me some good news. "Hello?"

"Good evening," he greets, even if slightly apprehensively. "Am I calling you too late?"

"Oh no, that's totally fine," I answer back, my tone dripping with enthusiasm. *Enough, Petra!*

"Well, I just wanted to let you know that I did speak to our client about your offer…" Oh my goodness! My heart is bouncing so damn hard inside my chest in anticipation of his next set of words.

"And?" I ask since he's taking way too long to finish his sentence.

"And unfortunately, as I was expecting, they have already started to refurbish the building and have other projects in mind for it. As I have said before, they really wanted that place in particular." My heart squeezes tight at the bad news, even though I already knew deep inside it was a lost cause since the day I spoke to him. "I just wanted to return your call as I said I would."

Well, I'm not sure if it was worth calling me just to tell me that, but in any case, I take a long, deep breath, and focus on keeping myself as cool as possible. "Thank you for calling me back," I manage to pull off. "It's fine, I figured they weren't interested anyway. I'll find another place." And I force myself to smile as I say those words, even though I know he can't see it.

"My apologies for not being able to deliver better news." He sounds quite sincere, but I don't find the will to reply. "Have a great evening."

"You too. Thanks," I mutter just before hanging up the call.

I shouldn't have been so insistent about that building. The truth is I became so emotionally attached to it that now every time I'm confronted with the reality that it's gonna become a restaurant, it hurts. Yes, it's a historic building in downtown Manhattan where the artistic soul of The Artemis

Room lives, but I'm sure I can find something else—something just as charming. I sigh, mentally putting this place in a grave once and for all. Rest in peace, my dear Artemis Room.

Knock, knock, knock.

I'm startled by the thumping sound, and before I can say a word, I see the door slowly opening and Alex standing behind it, peeking his head between the gap to check on me. "Is everything okay?" he asks gently, before coming in.

"Yeah," I say, my eyes drifting away as I'm still trying to digest the loss of my dear Artemis Room. "I was just talking to the new property manager of the building that I wanted to buy."

"Oh." His eyes widen in surprise. "And?"

"And the new owners aren't interested in selling it," I tell him, before blowing out a breath. "Not even for double. It's crazy."

"Double?" he repeats, visibly shocked as he stands before me. "It's even crazier you were so ready to pay double for it, Petra."

His comment resonates with me and I'm left a bit regretful to have wanted to offer them so much more than its current market worth. "I know, but that place was really the perfect one for my gallery."

"Don't you think you are exaggerating a bit?" he asks, gently stroking my cheek to bring my attention back to him. "Sometimes we don't get what we want in life, and that's okay. It happens."

"Yeah, but the hardest part is trying to accept it and move on." I cut eye contact, my eyes dropping to the floor again.

Silence emerges between us as Alex seems to be thinking something through. "Do you want to go somewhere this weekend?" he asks out of nowhere. "It's your birthday weekend after all."

Oh, talking about birthday plans won't help much to ease my pain, but I give him a smile in return. It's really sweet of him to try to lift my mood like that. I press my lips together and consider his question. "Honestly, just a date with the two of us would be fine."

"Anything you have particularly in mind?" he keeps asking.

I shrug, pondering further. "Maybe a romantic dinner, followed by a play, and…" My gaze goes up again, meeting his piercing blue eyes.

"And?"

Oh dear, and I forgot what I was about to say. A thousand naughty thoughts play in my head and I wet my lips, putting myself on my tip toes so that I can whisper in his ear. "We could have a sleepover in a nice hotel somewhere, just the two of us."

The corner of his lips curve up, forming a devilish sexy smile, most likely picturing the same as I. "Duly noted," he says matching my low tone, before pressing those delicious lips on mine for a much-needed kiss. "Now, what if we go and decorate that Christmas tree?"

CHAPTER 9

Petra

"We're going to be late for dinner!" Alex yells up the stairs from the foyer, and I growl to myself, pawing through my jewelry box for the right pair of earrings.

"I said I'm coming!" I shout back, cursing my husband under my breath.

When Alex asked what I wanted to do for my twentieth birthday a few days ago, I had told him what I wanted most was a date with him, maybe a dinner and a play followed by a night spent in a nice hotel room, away from all the craziness of our day-to-day lives.

He had agreed, but now that the day had arrived, I'm feeling rushed and flustered. The twins are teething, and they have regressed to crying on and off throughout the night for the past two days, meaning they had both been grouchy little handfuls for the past forty-eight hours. At 5 pm, Alex had casually dropped the bomb that he had gotten us a reservation at Blue Hill at Stone Barns, a farm-to-table restaurant with vast tasting menus and two Michelin stars—it also happens to be located very close to our home in Bedford Hills...

But it is for 6 pm!

With such short notice, I had all but run to the shower, scrubbing the day's sweat from my hair, and bolting from under the spray straight to my vanity to start my makeup, hair still dripping down my back. I apply my products, ending with a natural, dewy look accented by shimmering highlighter and barely there taupe eyeshadow.

In all honesty, I had been so consumed painting in my atelier that I hadn't remembered that it was my birthday until around two pm, and I had seen the date printed on the newspaper Alex had left on the dining room table. My husband had given no hints that he recalled the significance of the day until he sprang the dinner surprise on me. It figures that Alex would remember when I couldn't.

My long dark-brown hair has air-dried into gentle waves, so I plait my bangs back from my face and secure them with a delicate diamond clip, matching it with my diamond teardrop earrings. My neckline comes nearly to my throat, so I decide to skip the necklace, choosing to only be adorned by the Chantilly Lace of the sheath dress. It ends at my knees, and the slip underneath is a nude illusion, so it almost appears that I am wearing nothing but a delicate lace layer.

I take a step back, slipping my feet into my nude heels, and look my reflection over. For getting ready in less than thirty minutes, I look pretty incredible. Pregnancy had widened my hips and filled out my bust just a smidge, and my tiny bit of extra curvature really makes my dress pop.

I make my way down the hall to the nursery, heels clicking rhythmically on the floor, to tell Lily and the babies goodnight. Alex hadn't mentioned if we'd stay in Bedford Hills to spend the night, but he'd have to have given Lily the scoop if she was going to be on baby duty all evening.

"Hey everyone," I call quietly, creeping into the room in case the twins are sleeping.

In fact, they are both bright-eyed and awake. We had bought an array of musical toys for them recently, and they are sitting on each side of a rainbow wooden xylophone. Jasper slaps at the metal bars with his hands while Jasmine tries, with all of her limited motor skills, to tap at them with the attached mallet.

Lily has been picking the room up since I entered, and she raises her eyebrows when she gets a good look at me. "I'm guessing you're going out?" she asks, wiping her hands.

"Alex didn't tell you?" I respond, suddenly worried that he had forgotten to inform Lily, but she shakes her head.

"Oh, no, he did. I just wasn't sure you'd go on such short notice." Lily beams at me, clasping her hands together. "You're going to have such a great time!"

Her reaction is odd, almost like she's overly excited. "Uh, it's just dinner."

"Sure, sure," she snaps. "Well, get out of here, birthday girl! You don't want to be late!" She motions towards the door and bizarrely, I feel like I'm being rushed out of my own nursery.

"Hold on! I wanted to tell the twins goodnight," I say, ignoring Lily's instructions to leave.

I lower myself to the ground with the babies, and they both immediately drop what they're doing to come to me. Jasper is able to take a few shaky crawling steps forward, and though Jasmine can lift herself up for a couple of seconds, she still needs to fall to her belly, pulling herself across the floor with her arms.

I scoop them up one by one, saving them the effort of coming to me, and kiss both of their soft, warm cheeks before snuggling them close. "I'll miss you two, be good for Lily."

"Ma ma," Jasmine breathes when I pull her to me. "Ma ma ma ma ma."

Her words, intentional or not, give me a lump in my throat. I love these little humans so much that it takes my breath away sometimes. I hesitate to put her down while Jasper curls up on my lap, and for a moment I consider kicking my heels off and canceling the whole birthday dinner. This is where I wanted to be most of all.

"Petra," Lily's voice breaks through my thoughts. "You're going to miss your reservation."

I exhale, plopping my daughter back on the play rug, and untangle myself from my son's limbs, standing up and straightening my dress. "I guess you're right…"

"You're going to have a great time. Really," Lily assures me, walking me to the nursery door. "Don't worry about a thing with these two. I'll you see tomorrow."

I take one last look at the twins before turning towards the stairs. This better be the best dinner in existence, for how quickly I had to get ready, not to mention leaving my babies for an unknown period of time with no forewarning.

I take the stairs slowly in my stilettos, and when I see Alex, dressed sharply in a navy-blue suit and no tie, he's anxiously checking his watch. He breathes a sigh of relief when he sees me, before looking me over with barely concealed interest in his eyes.

"Well, we're going to be late, but if you look like that, I guess it was worth it," he tells me, his voice rough and intimate as I approach him.

I do a full turn, letting him see every inch of me, and he makes a noise somewhere between a curse and a growl. "I've never been angrier at myself for making an early reservation."

With a breathy laugh, I slither my way into his arms. His gaze is heated, but his jaw is set stubbornly. He had made up his mind about how the evening was going to go. I settle for a quick peck on his soft lips before walking around him to grab my coat. I decide on a long, cream-colored trench coat, something that I never would have worn while going out with the kids. No better time than now!

I link my arm through Alex's, letting him steady me as we walk to the car. I expect his usual black Mercedes-Benz, but what I see idling on the curb isn't our usual car. Alex has taken the freaking Rolls Royce out of storage, and it purrs in front of our condo, looking sleek and almost predatory.

"The Rolls Royce? Why?" I ask him, bewildered. "It's just a birthday dinner."

Alex gives me a knowing look. "Just let me pull out all the stops for my beautiful wife, okay? Now, get in."

I blow out a breath. Something about Alex's behavior, combined with the late notice about the dinner and Lily's equally strange behavior, sets an alarm off in the back of my mind. Is he hiding something from me?

I squint at him, pursing my lips. "You're up to something."

He grins like a Cheshire cat, as he opens the rear door of the car for me. "Even if I was, I wouldn't tell you. Now get in."

"Fine. But I'm on to you." I crawl into the car, flipping on the heated seats immediately and sinking into the buttery quilted leather.

"Ready?" Alex asks, a devious glint in his ocean-blue eyes as he comes and sits beside me. I nod curtly, and Zach, the chauffeur, pulls the brilliant machine onto the road.

Traffic in Manhattan is garbage, as usual, but we have enough moments on the open road that I can really enjoy the power of the car.

"How far is this place?" I ask, watching the city lights race by us.

"Closer than you think," he responds coyly.

We drive for twenty minutes, Zach guiding the car masterfully through the late evening rush, but the direction he's going seems all wrong for our destination. I've never been to Blue Hill at Stone Barns, but Zach seems to be taking us deeper into the city instead of towards the outskirts. The place had the word *barn* in it, for goodness sake. It couldn't be in a high rise.

"What's going on?" I ask again, sitting up straight in my seat. "Alex, this isn't funny. I haven't eaten since breakfast, and that was just a grapefruit."

"If you ask again, I'm taking you back home," he snarks. I groan and slide back in my seat, crossing my arms.

Eventually, Zach flicks on the turn signal, sliding the Rolls Royce effortlessly up to a valet station. I take a second to realize where we are, but when it hits me, I grab Alex's arm before he can exit the car, my grip tight. I can't believe what I'm seeing out of the car window right now. No way!

"No. I don't want to eat here. Please take me home," I beg, feeling heartsick. Why would Alex play a joke like this?

Alex shakes me off without responding, while Zach is already handing the car keys to the wide-eyed teenage valet. Alex makes his way to my side of the car and after opening my door, he reaches his hand down to help me out, but my arms remain stubbornly crossed against my chest.

"You have to face this, Petra. I know it's still bothering you," Alex insists sternly.

"I don't care. This is cruel and you know it!" I lash out, but instead of giving me a cutting remark back, he kneels down, turning my face to his with a gentle touch.

"Do you really think I would hurt you purposely on your birthday? Do you think that little of me, my sweet wife?"

My anger deflates at the hurt look in his gaze, and despite everything in me screaming to do otherwise, I take his hand when he offers it to me again. I can feel my bottom lip quivering, and Alex takes notice, stroking my cheek with his knuckles and kissing my shaky lip.

"Don't cry. Trust me, okay? Just have a little faith here, little Petra," he murmurs quietly, bumping his nose against mine.

I can see the valet awkwardly shifting from foot to foot while he waits on us. No matter how out of control I feel at this moment, I have to trust Alex as he says. I have no other option.

I give him a swift nod, not wanting to speak. Alex slips his arm through mine and leads me, like a starlet walking down the red carpet, up the vast concrete stairs into the formerly named Artemis Room.

My fingers dig into his arm harder with each step. I can hear the liveliness inside but can't see a thing because of the curtains being drawn. The outdoor lighting is almost theatrical, with different shades of white and gold illuminating the flourishes on the handsome stone. It's dusk, and I try to get a closer look, realizing that the new owners had power washed the place, restoring it to its former grandeur. The two gargoyles perched on the top cornerstones gleamed almost white in the spotlights shining underneath them, their hideous visages glaring out at the city beyond.

"Do you approve of what they've done with the place?" Alex asks me, pausing midway so we can get a full look at the building. I have to admit, it looks a million times better than the dark, mossy appearance it had sported just a few weeks ago.

"Reluctantly yes. I was afraid there would be an enormous neon sign bolted above the entrance or something," I admit. "But I just realized that there aren't any indications of what this place is. How will people even know it's a restaurant?"

Alex chuckles under his breath. "It's a soft opening. I managed to score us an invitation. You're a VIP, after all."

We continue walking towards the doors when I fully process his explanation. I plant my feet, stopping him. "What do you mean, I'm a VIP?"

He looks exasperated, tilting his face to the darkening sky and exhaling, his breath misting in the cold air. "If you would quit dragging your feet, you would know already. Come on!"

He tugs me forward with uncharacteristic vigor. Alex, usually stoic and unflappable, is antsy about something. Now I'm absolutely positive something weird is going on.

I open my mouth to question him when two doormen stationed outside pull open the enormous French doors for us, illuminating our path. I swallow hard. I refuse to cry when we go in. At least they preserved the outside. Maybe the inside wouldn't be terrible.

With a steadying breath, I let Alex lead me into the building, and thank goodness he is with me because without his arm around me I might have fallen to the floor when, with a jolt, I absorb what I'm seeing.

Instead of high top tables, the glistening white marble floors are bare, and instead of kitschy brick-and-brack, the pale gray walls are adorned with... with...

With my paintings!

Not just my own, either. The special pieces I had collected over the years are hung as well, including our beloved piece from Pierre Soulages.

Here and there, concrete pillars stand, holding busts and carvings I had found striking, each illuminated by a low-hanging light overhead. Geez, it's exactly how I had imagined my gallery would look. Except now it's right in front of me.

And it's mine.

Before I can even find the right words, my eyes filling with tears, the coup de grâce comes.

"SURPRISE! Happy birthday, Petra!" everyone I love screams, pouring out from behind the grand staircase.

I slap my hands over my mouth, unable to contain the sob of joy that escapes. As my friends and family flow around me, my husband grabs me around the waist, hauling me off my feet and spinning us in a quick circle before I'm dipped down like a ballroom dancer. He flashes a triumphant smile before fastening his mouth over mine.

The crowd around us cheers, and when Alex pulls away, he whispers against my lips, "Happy birthday, little Petra."

In stunned silence, I explore my new gallery. Alex leaves me to my party guests, disappearing into the crowd, but he's replaced at my side almost immediately by Emma, who looks like a beautiful, sophisticated badass tonight. Her shoulder-length, jet-black hair is tied in a conservative chignon on the back of her head, and her green A-line dress is so dark that it's almost black. Instead of dress shoes, she's wearing a spotless pair of patent leather Balenciaga's. Her neckline dips low, and her butterfly chest tattoo rivals some of the paintings on the wall in intricacy.

"Be honest with me," she starts, sidling up beside me while we chat. "Did you have any idea?"

"Not an inkling of anything like this. I can't believe Alex pulled this off. It's... I don't even know. I'm at a loss." I hold my hands up helplessly.

"You must fuck him senseless for him to love you *this* much," Emma gestures around the room, dodging the swat I try to give her for the filthy commentary.

"That's none of your business," I hiss to her, and she waggles her perfect eyebrows at me suggestively.

"Maybe he told me so," Emma continues.

I snort. "I think *not*. Good try, though. Can we look at the gallery now, you pervert?"

"If you insist," she sighs.

With my best friend at my side, I peruse every inch of the place, my brain struggling to take in everything I'm seeing. Alex has managed to arrange my paintings by age, from my blunt, primary-colored attempts as a preteen all the way up to my most recent piece, the large slice-of-life painting depicting the autumn trees and cardinals in Central Park. I didn't even notice he had taken it out of the atelier to hang it here.

I sniffle, dashing my errant tears away as they spill over. Everything has been done with so much thoughtfulness and so much care. I can't even fathom the time and organization that it must have taken to accomplish this in such a short period of time.

Emma draws me into a one-armed hug when I come to stand in front of a very special painting, situated directly in the middle of the display. It's my first painting, the one that I had finally been able to gift to Alex after we had announced my pregnancy to my dad. It's the scene that I had painted of

Alex and myself, and miraculously of the twins as well. I had only been a seven-year-old girl when I put the scene to canvas, but somehow, my heart already knew my future.

"Hold it together," Emma advises, seeing that I'm about to burst into uncontrollable tears.

She steers me away from the special painting, chattering about some of the pieces by other artists until I regain my composure. I give her a watery smile and forcing my brain to focus on something else, I ask, "Any update on our little, um, background check?"

"Still digging, my dear, still digging." She pats my shoulder reassuringly. "Don't worry, before Christmas I should have an entire dossier about her." We stop in front of another wall filled with artwork, our backs to the crowd. "Are you good now?"

I nod at her, straightening my posture.

Emma leans closer to my ear and then looking to her left side, she says, "Thank goodness, because some of these people look like they might explode if you don't speak to them soon."

I follow her gaze and I find Matt, and to my astonishment his dad Eric, hanging out near the concessions table. The father and son duo look tense, and an expression of relief flits over Matt's face when he sees us.

"Petra! Emma! Over here!" he calls, causing Eric to scoff.

Matt moves as if he wants to hug us, but at the last minute remembers his dad is watching, so for some weird reason, he just shakes our hands awkwardly. I hold out my hand for Eric to shake, but he refuses to look down, pretending to not see my offer of a greeting hanging in the air.

"Your husband must truly enjoy making the headlines to have invited so many reporters," Eric comments rudely, craning his neck to look over the place. "Good luck with the gallery."

I scowl, but Eric bids us a brusque farewell, not bothering to look any of us in the eye. Once he is gone from sight, Matt relaxes, a clear weight falling away from him. He blows out a breath and scratches the top of his head.

"Sorry about that, I don't even know why he came if it was to behave like that," Matt says, his voice filled with apology.

"Because he knows it's a big event and it will be noticed if he doesn't show his face, at least for a little while. Classic narcissist bullshit," Emma says with disdain, crossing her arms.

"You're not wrong," Matt admits.

He hugs each of us now, and I can't help but notice that when he pulls away from Emma, his eyes linger on the tattoo gracing her chest and collarbones. Matt coughs and turns his head, but not before I see the redness flushing his face. Poor guy, he is barking up the wrong tree for sure.

"Where's Sarah?" I ask for the sake of politeness.

"Oh, she went to the bathroom," he answers promptly, before changing the subject. "I'd have gotten you a gift, but your husband insisted it wasn't necessary. We all made donations to the Turner Syndrome foundation instead," he comments, loading his plate with some appetizers from the concessions table.

"That's incredible! Thank you," I tell him sincerely. "Have you seen my dad by any chance?"

"Your dad and Catherine are around here somewhere," Matt continues. "I don't know half of these people though, so I couldn't tell you who they were with."

"Thanks for the tip, Matt. I'm going to go track him and my husband down. I'll catch up with you guys in a bit?"

Emma nods. "I need a cigarette anyway, I'm headed outside."

"Yuck, but okay. I'm gonna check on Sarah. See you guys in a bit." I give them a brief wave, popping a few pieces of fruit into my mouth from the catering table before braving the crowd once more.

After the burst of energy of the initial surprise, people separated into smaller groups to check out the artwork. Alex had found some of the original artists as well, and they stand in front of their artwork, answering questions and networking with the guests and reporters.

I make a point to greet each and every artist that came to the opening. After all, I'd admired their art for so long and it fills me with fierce pride to see them here in my gallery. This is why I'd created the art fund, to give a voice to those who had been long ignored in the art world. My gallery would be the platform these brilliant artists needed.

Ms. Artemis had been well-intentioned, filling the need for a community-ran gallery all those decades ago when The Artemis Room first opened, but after many years in the art scene, she had begun to feature her friends more often than not, until The Artemis Room was simply a revolving gallery of the same ten or so artists.

I swore to myself I would never fall into that pattern. In my gallery, the walls would always feature someone new. This place wasn't just for me, it was for artists all over New York and beyond. Soon, I'm positive that everyone will be flocking to... to... wait. What is the gallery even called?

"Hey, kid," a deep voice says from behind me. I turn quickly, letting myself be wrapped in my dad's embrace. "Happy birthday, and all that."

"Did you have anything to do with this?" I ask him when he releases me.

He chuckles. "Sort of. Once Alex gets his mind locked in on something, there is no convincing him otherwise. I told him to store all of your things at my place until the gallery was ready, and he's dragged me through here a few times. But really, it was mostly him. He wanted to do this for you."

"It's beyond anything I ever expected," I admit.

"Don't just look at it as a present, now. This is a gift and an investment," he says excitedly. "You're going to have to put your blood, sweat, and tears into this place, just like Alex did to get it ready for you. Are you able to do that and finish college at the same time?" Dad asks me, sounding quite serious.

"Yes, of course," I answer resolutely. "I'll have a team to help so I'm pretty sure I can do both."

Dad smiles proudly. "Great." Then he pauses for a beat as he seems to be thinking something through. "Catherine wanted to see you. Would you mind saying hello to her?"

My brows raise instantly at his request. "Still with her, huh?" I ask teasingly.

"She's a good friend," he answers, remaining just as vague as the first time he introduced me to her. "Come over, she'll be delighted." I follow him as we cross the gallery, passing through a few familiar faces, until we find Ms. Dubois, with a glass of champagne in one hand, surrounded by a few artists as she delights them with her pleasantries and good manners. While they seem all smitten about her, I take a moment to admire her long, elegant black dress filled with embroideries and feathers. I wonder why she is wearing black again. Is she grieving the loss of someone or is it just her favorite color? A question I don't think is appropriate to ask in front of my dad.

"Congratulations," Catherine says, a perfect white smile on display as she finally looks in our direction. "I knew you were a painter, but I never thought you had such a vast portfolio at such a young age. You truly have a gift."

"Thank you," I reply politely before we exchange two cheek kisses.

"This is such a beautiful set-up," she praises, glancing around the room, before wetting her lips with the champagne. "I also used to paint when I was younger. I mean, when I was in my thirties or so."

"Oh, really?" Geez! I know that painting is a popular hobby, but damn, the fact she used to paint just like my mom still makes me a bit uncomfortable. As I come to think of it, from their hobbies to their physical appearances, Mom and Catherine are so freaking similar that I'm starting to believe that this is just a way for Dad to cope with his ex-wife's death. Or is it just a simple coincidence? Who knows! I have so many questions to ask him, but now is definitely not the right moment or place to do so.

"Yes, oil painting too, but mostly still life," she adds, my attention returning to her. "Nothing worth hanging in a gallery though."

"Well, you never know," I reply. "New artists tend to undervalue their work, but I can assure you there's value even in the very first painting."

"I saw the first painting you did," she says, her smile growing as she keeps observing me. "What an incredible little girl you were."

I give her a smile in return, not knowing what else to say, despite her compliment.

"What's the name of the gallery by the way?" Catherine asks me, most likely to change the subject of our conversation.

"That's a good question," I answer, before looking at my dad. "Hey, Dad? Do you know what Alex decided to call the place?"

He frowns. "You mean you didn't read the engraving before you came in?"

I grimace. "Uh, no. He had me thinking we were coming to see the new restaurant that was supposedly being built here. My eyes were locked straight ahead."

"Risky. He's lucky you even came in! Here, come with me."

Dad leads me through the gallery towards the entrance. The atmosphere of the building is jovial, with everyone making their way around and talking. I can only hope that every opening I host will go as well as this one.

When we emerge into the cold night air, Dad motions for me to look at the copper-colored engraved plaque bolted to the wall next to the entrance. I lean down to read, my grin growing with each letter.

The Gatt-Dieren Gallery
Gifted to a Beloved Wife and Mother,
To Uplift the Artists of New York City

"It's perfect," I whisper, blinking rapidly so the tears don't start anew.

Dad pats me on the back. "I knew you'd like it."

"Where is Alex, anyway?" I ask with a sniffle.

Dad shrugs. "I only saw him for a moment. He said he was putting the finishing touches on the second floor."

The second floor! In all the excitement, I had totally forgotten about the offices on the upper floor. Surely Alex hadn't had time to renovate them yet, but it didn't matter to me one bit. After all the hard work he had fed into the gallery portion of the building, I could definitely handle arranging the revamp of the offices.

"I'm going to go find him, then. It's so like him to drop a gift like this and then disappear."

I check the time: seven pm, so I make a pit stop to call Lily and check up on the twins. She's just finished their nightly bath routine and is preparing to lay them down. I fill her in on how the surprise went, and how incredible the gallery is.

Afterward, I hang up and head back inside, my eyes already on the grand staircase that leads to the second floor. The top floor is dark, and I feel strange leaving my own birthday party, but everyone is occupied and enjoying themselves. There's really no reason for me to remain downstairs for now, so I'll just find Alex and drag him back to the party. He deserves to enjoy the opening, too.

No one seems to take notice as I climb the stairs, my hand gliding across the polished wooden railing that has been smoothed down by the passing of hundreds of hands over the years.

Two hallways branch off on the left and right at the top of the stairs, both completely dark. I can see the outline of the antique stained glass light fixtures at even intervals on the ceiling, but not a single one is turned on. Maybe Alex isn't here after all?

I start to head back down when I notice the glow of a single light underneath a closed office door. I can't imagine why Alex would hide himself up here, but my curiosity gets the better of me and I go to investigate. I rap on the door three times.

"Alex?" I call softly, my hand already twisting the handle.

"You don't have to knock on the door of your own office, you know," he responds from the other side.

I push the door open, and there is my husband, sitting on the corner of a brand-new computer desk. I barely have time to register all the furniture in the office when I notice something out of place: a bottle of Dom Pérignon chilling in an ice bucket next to Alex, and the two champagne flutes he holds upside down by the stems in one hand.

"Drinking up here all by yourself?" I tease, leaning on the door frame.

His lips twist into one hell of a sexy smile and he stands up. "Not quite." Then he puts the glasses down on the desk, before carefully opening the bottle and filling them each with a hefty portion of the champagne. "I was waiting on you to start drinking, actually." He holds out one flute to me, and when I saunter slowly over to him, I can see the gleam of lust in his cerulean gaze. It seems we might do a little bit more than drink to celebrate...

"How did you know I would come upstairs to check?"

"Because I know you," he answers softly, before raising up his glass. "Cheers," he tells me, his voice thick, and we clink our glasses together.

The champagne bubbles on my tongue, acidic and bright with hints of vanilla that denote its quality. I close my eyes and savor it slowly before tilting the glass back to finish it, setting the flute on the desk with a "clink."

Alex is pulling me towards him, his large hands on my hips, but I can't help looking around the place. The hallway floors had been the same marble as the gallery, but this office had brand new low pile carpet to muffle sound and a fresh coat of pale sage paint. The desk is empty beside Alex, and it's sleekly modern with loads of storage space. On the floor by the door is a big cardboard box emblazoned with the telltale Apple logo, indicating a brand-new Mac.

Somehow, Alex had taken care of the upstairs, too. The whole building seems to be ready to go as soon as I want.

"How did you even accomplish this?" I ask in awe. "I have so many questions."

"Hmm," he murmurs, pulling me closer still so I could feel his breath tickling my neck. "Can the questions wait until later?"

I melt into him, letting him drag his lips from my nape to the shell of my ear. "Just tell me one thing—how did you convince Nico to buy the building when he wouldn't give me the time of day?"

"Business moguls have to keep their secrets," he says, taunting me even more.

"I'm not buying it."

"Fine, Ms. Curiosity. Turns out our friend, Nico Tucci, hadn't been keeping up on his property taxes for the last few years, and delinquent taxes stay with the building under new ownership. Hakkasan Group had no idea how much was really owed, and they put a hold on the purchase once someone gave them an anonymous tip," Alex smirks. "Nico was more than happy to sell to me when he realized that if he didn't sell the gallery asap, *he* would be stuck with the taxes, especially since the city officials were already drawing up the paperwork for criminal nonpayment."

"That's devious," I gasp. "You'd be so mean to that poor, old landlord?" I ask teasingly.

"I'd be mean to anyone if it meant making you as happy as you are tonight." He drags his knuckles over my cheekbone. "But I must say, I'm quite impressed that you even tried to reach the new owners. Your determination never ceases to amaze me."

My face falls a little with my next thought. "I still feel like I failed a bit, though. I should have been able to close the deal on my own."

Alex shakes his head in disagreement. "Your offer was good, but sometimes to win a deal you need to go above and beyond and be more creative. That's why getting to know the darkest secrets of your adversary gives you the upper hand."

I nod in understanding. "Yeah, I should've done that," I admit. "That was a brilliant move."

"I agree," he replies, his voice steady. "Plus, by purchasing it, I help retain some of the city's historical architecture while you funnel grant money into local up-and-coming artists. Sounds like a good investment."

I groan, touching my forehead to his. "My dad said the exact same thing."

Alex chuckles under his breath. "We're business partners for a reason."

"That's all well and good, but I so don't want to be thinking about my dad right now."

Alex sits back some, refilling my champagne flute and handing it to me. "Wash the images away, then," he suggests.

I gladly take another drink of the pricy vintage, letting it tickle my nose as I do so. The sparkling wine is refreshing and cold, but the alcohol warms my belly from the inside out, making my head feel pleasantly fuzzy.

"Is it working?" Alex inquires, taking a swig directly from the bottle.

"Alex! Don't do that!" I exclaim with laughter, trying to take the bottle from him.

He dodges me, taking another swig before depositing the nearly empty bottle back into the ice bucket. "Greedy little thing," he comments, and I huff, acting like I'm going to storm out dramatically.

My ploy works, and he grabs me around the middle, dragging me back to him. "Hey, you're not going anywhere," he tells me, brushing my hair away from my shoulders and kissing the back of my neck along my hairline. "Not until we properly celebrate at least."

"I thought that's what we were doing downstairs," I say, my voice catching as I feel the swipe of his tongue over the pulse point on the side of my throat.

"This is more of a… private celebration," he rumbles, keeping one arm locked around me while the other slides my dress ever so slowly up my thighs. I'm suddenly very thankful that I didn't wear pantyhose tonight.

"If you insist," I breathe, shuddering at the feeling of the rough pads of his fingers trailing up my sensitive thighs.

"We have to christen the building obviously." Alex lightly sets his teeth into my skin, and it causes a whole-body shiver. "Since this will be your office, I want you thinking about what we did in here every time you sit down to work."

"That… that won't be a problem," I tell him, turning in his grasp until we are face to face.

I am drawn into him like a magnet, or like a meteor pulled into the gravity of the Earth. I couldn't resist this man, my husband, even if I tried.

I kiss him lightly at first, just a swift pass of lips, lingering longer and longer each time until I allow my tongue to dart out to taste him. Alex makes a little grunt in his chest, slanting his mouth over mine and deepening the kiss.

He explores my mouth languorously, at the pace of someone who knows exactly what they're doing. Heat rises in me from the tips of my toes to pool in my stomach, molten and burning, and I lean into Alex hard. I can't get enough of him.

Eventually, he breaks the kiss. I examine his face, taking in his pupils that are blown wide with lust and the way he pants with need as if he had been running a marathon instead of making out with his wife. I'm overcome by a rush of pure affection and make a swift decision.

"Let me thank you for this," I purr, my hands falling to the buttons of his shirt as I begin to undo them.

"Thank me how, exactly?" he asks, jaw tight.

"I think you know how," I respond, undoing the last button and opening his shirt wide, exposing the bronze skin of his chest and the hard planes of his muscles. I run my hands over him hungrily.

"Say it," Alex commands, no trace of humor in his voice now.

"I want to thank you by... by..." I might be a married woman with two kids, but I'm still not over the fact my husband wants me to be that graphic with him. I take a deep breath, gain some courage, and lean slightly closer to his ear, just in case someone else could hear me. "Sucking your cock here in my new office." I force the words out, feeling simultaneously embarrassed and turned on.

Alex stands, working at the belt on his pants until they fall to the floor. His erection is pressing hard against his black boxer shorts, begging to be touched. I swallow hard, reaching my hand out to caress him, feeling the iron rod of his cock waiting for me right behind this one single layer.

"Dress off, but leave the heels on," Alex instructs, his voice having dropped to nearly a growl.

"You'll have to help me unzip it then." I turn around and he grasps the zipper, pulling it down steadily until my dress is gaping open in the back. I slide my arms from the sleeves and let the dress pool at my feet, leaving me in nothing but a matching set of white lace bra and panties.

I try to turn back around, but Alex's hands move to the clasp of my bra, tracing the edge of the lace with his fingers before unhooking it completely, sliding the straps down my shoulders, and tossing the undergarment aside. He reaches around me, palming my tits and rolling my nipples between his fingers as I suck in a stuttering breath, the sensations going straight from my nipples to the needy place between my legs.

"I'm supposed to be thanking you, not the other way around," I protest weakly, pressing my breasts into his hands.

"All in due time, wife," he replies.

I want so desperately to turn and kiss him or to sink to my knees and pleasure him, but Alex doesn't let me move, alternating between circling my hard peaks with his fingers and pinching them lightly until I'm a mess, my head thrown back and moans falling from my mouth without hesitation.

I can't take much more. I either need to touch him or have him inside of me. Just as I'm about to protest, Alex's hands fall away from my chest, and he turns me with a firm hand on my shoulder. "What was it you were saying about thanking me?"

I almost want to pout about being teased so mercilessly, but I think better of it, lowering myself to my knees as planned and slipping my fingers under the waistband of his briefs, tugging them down. His erection pops free from the shorts, bobbing in the air until I wrap my hand around the base of it.

Alex is watching me like a hawk as I bring my mouth to him, darting my tongue out to lick the droplet of precum gracing the tip. He blows out a breath between his teeth, cupping the back of my head with his palm to hold me in place.

He shouldn't have bothered. There was no place on Earth that I wanted to be except for right here, right now.

Running my hands up his muscled thighs, I grip him while I take his manhood into my mouth, loosening my jaw so I can fit as much of his considerable length as possible. When I can go no further, I make up the rest of the length with my hand, pumping him a few times experimentally before finding a steady rhythm with both my hands and mouth.

Alex hisses before letting his head fall back, eyes fixed on the ceiling and the fingers of his right hand buried in my hair, guiding me with gentle pressure to please him just the way he likes it.

It's exhilarating knowing the door is unlocked and being able to hear the sounds of the party filtering in as he and I share this private moment. I revel in the taste of Alex, the feeling of him bumping into the back of my throat, and the restrained noises he continues to make for me.

I could have kept going, but when I swirl my tongue around the head of his member over and over, he grips my hair harder than before and holds me still, cursing under his breath. "Enough."

He pulls himself from my mouth with a wet pop. "But —"

"I said enough," he insists, helping me to my feet.

My legs feel wobbly from the extended time spent on my knees, but Alex doesn't give me any time to catch my breath. Instead, he pulls aside my lace panties and slips a finger between my folds, causing me to jump and steady myself with my hands on his shoulders.

"Did sucking me off get you nice and wet, Petra?" he asks, still probing me with his wandering fingers. "Tell me."

"Yes," I bite out, and he grins wickedly.

"Good. I'm going to bend you over the desk and fuck you senseless now. Is that what you want?"

"Ye—es," I cry out as he circles my clit with the pad of his thumb. I have to dig my fingers into his shoulders hard to stop from losing my balance. He's driving me wild with just the smallest touches, and I'm completely at his mercy. "Yes Alex, please."

"Well," he starts. "Because you asked so nicely, I think I can oblige."

He pulls his hand out from between my thighs, yanking my panties down in one smooth motion so I can step out of them. I'm now completely nude besides my stilettos, and my skin is pebbling in the chill office air—causing me to feel exposed but deliciously hot all over. My core is throbbing with anticipation of what's to come.

"You're beautiful," Alex tells me sweetly, before stepping away from the desk and waving an arm toward it. "Now why don't you bend over here and show me that pretty ass of yours too?"

"Okay," I breathe, my heart fluttering in my chest.

We're really going to do this! He's really going to fuck me right here in my new office!

There could be no better way to mark the place as our own.

He, completely nude and looking no less intimidating for it, watches me with his arms crossed as I assume the position he has requested of me, bending over the shining new desk, my ass on full display for him.

"Just like that," he murmurs, his tone suffused with heat.

The polished wood of the desk is cold on my stomach and breasts, and I shiver, but I'm soon warmed by Alex's body as he stretches out above me, his hands planted on the desk. I feel the heat radiating off of him, soothing my chilled flesh.

He starts by kissing a line down my spine until he reaches the two dimples right above my butt, where he stops to swirl his tongue around each one. He spends an equal amount of time on the globes of my ass cheeks before slipping two fingers between my legs and dipping them into the well of my pussy. I moan, twitching beneath his hands in surprise.

"Look at how ready you are for me, Petra," he says darkly.

I am panting with need as he fingers me, every few minutes stopping to spank me with a quick slap. He curls his fingers deep inside of me, and I'm almost seeing stars from how incredible it feels.

"Please," I beg, more than ready for him to fuck me.

Everything else has left my brain, and the only thing I can concentrate on through the fog of lust is Alex, his hands on me, and his deep voice giving praise. The rest of the world falls away, leaving only the two of us.

The pleasure he is giving me coils in my belly like a thundercloud, ready to burst at any moment. His fingers feel amazing stroking my inner walls, but it just isn't enough. I press my forehead against the cool wood of the desk and groan, all at once so frustrated but so aroused.

Finally, Alex pulls his fingers from me, and for a second I almost cry out in annoyance at the vast empty feeling he leaves behind. I don't have to worry for too much time though. His long fingers are replaced by the thick head of his cock, pressing between my folds, and resting at the mouth of my womanhood, not penetrating me but letting me know exactly what's to follow.

There are a thousand things I would like to say. I could plead, I could demand he slide into me, or I could groan his name to the empty walls. Instead, I say nothing, holding my breath for fear that if I said anything at all, he would pull away and start the tortuous foreplay all over again. As much as I love foreplay, I'm more than ready for the main event.

With one hand Alex holds onto my hip, keeping me in place, while the other is wrapped around his shaft as he guides himself with agonizing slowness into me. "Easy," he grates out when I buck underneath him.

I bite my lip, toes curling in my heels. I want him now, but Alex has made it abundantly clear that he is setting the pace. He fills me centimeter by aching centimeter, until, after the longest minutes of my life, he is rested completely inside of me, the bones of his hips pressing into the soft cushion of my ass and the head of his cock kissing my womb.

"So fucking tight," he growls, and the sound of it reaches the bottom of my soul.

We've done this hundreds of times before, but I'm still breathless at how fully he fills me, and how my inner walls clamp down on him like a glove.

After we adjust to each other, Alex finally takes mercy on me and moves, feeding himself into me with a steady, unceasing rhythm while I writhe under him, desperate to meet his thrusts as he bottoms out over and over.

I can hear his breath escaping between his teeth, and I feel the tenseness of his legs as he fills me, angling his hips so he pushes against that secret spot inside my pussy that has me nearly sobbing with joy. A jolt of deep pleasure flares each time, growing the storm inside of me more powerful by the second.

I all but howl his name, my eyes scrunched shut, the only other sounds in the room our ragged breathing and the erotic slaps of his flesh against mine. I suck in deep gulps of air, my body arching unconsciously as Alex drives me closer and closer to the edge. I just need something more, and then I'm going to topple over that edge.

"Oh, Alex! I'm almost there, almost—" I can hardly speak, but Alex knows me and knows what my body needs instinctually.

He slides one of his hands from my hip to the place where we meet, parting my swollen nether lips to find the small pearl of my clit. Alex uses his fingers to put pressure on either side of it, rubbing up and down, and it's like a lightning bold burning through me.

Where the liquid pleasure building in my stomach and spine had churned like an oncoming storm, his fingers between my legs were all the catalyst that storm needed to explode. And explode I did.

I push back into him fiercely as the rolling waves of my orgasm cascade over me, wracking my whole body with shivers. My inner walls clench down hard on Alex, and I hear him make a strangled noise behind me, his thrusts growing harder and more unsteady as he chases his own peak.

The climax starts anew when I feel him spill himself inside of me in a hot rush. He presses himself punishingly hard against me as he comes, his grip on my hips like iron.

Slowly, we both come down from our mutual highs. Alex almost collapses on top of me, bracketing my head with his elbows as his trim body covers mine. He peppers the side of my face, shoulders, and neck in exhausted kisses while we catch our breath, and remain motionless for a while, savoring the moment.

"Do we have to go back downstairs?" I ask sleepily, wanting nothing more than to stay here.

Alex grunts. "Unfortunately, yes. It's still your birthday party. You've got a cake coming, and if we don't return soon someone will probably call in a missing person report."

Frowning, I turn my head to the side to better see his face. "How long have we been up here?"

Alex checks his watch and winces. "Over an hour and a half."

"Alex!" I squeal, extricating myself from his embrace, scooping my undergarments and dress off the floor in a frantic rush. "I can't believe you kept me up here that long! Everyone is going to know what we were doing."

"So?" he shrugs. "Who cares if they know?"

I hook my bra back on, jerking the dress back over my head. Before I can step into the leg holes of my panties, I feel the warm drip of his cum running down my inner thigh. I feel my face flush while I ball the panties up in my fist. "Where is the bathroom?"

It turns out my office has its own attached bathroom, and I'm able to get myself cleaned up and my hair straightened enough that it isn't immediately obvious that my husband and I had been fornicating like rabbits during my birthday party. Once I'm cleaned up, I slip back into my underwear and return to the office to find Alex.

"Do I look presentable?" I ask him, turning in a slow circle.

He nods, and I stand on my tiptoes in front of him to straighten his collar. "You look perfect," he tells me. "Let's get back to this shindig before someone comes looking for us."

I'm startlingly self-conscious that I look messier than before, but Alex, of course, looks completely put together. It's almost infuriating how he could look so polished mere minutes after railing me against a desk in my office.

We descend the stone staircase arm in arm, and receive waves from a few guests, but nothing inflammatory enough to suggest they knew what we had been up to. It isn't until we're almost down to the main floor that I make eye contact with Emma, who is hanging with a group of alternatively dressed artists. She gives me an exaggerated wink before motioning to Alex, and I give her a death glare, but she pays it no mind, returning to her conversation.

"Wow," Alex comments, having seen the exchange.

"Don't... She must have been drinking." I say with a roll of my eyes.

At the bottom of the stairs, Alex and I split off. It's clear the party is winding down, and there is only one more event that has to take place before the night is over. The birthday cake.

One of the caterers wheels out a white trolly holding a cake that is covered by a protective lid. Everyone gathers around and I fidget, feeling oddly nervous about being the center of attention. I take a steadying breath and stand beside the trolley while the caterer removes the lid with a flourish.

My birthday cake is a three-tiered, semi-naked green matcha cake with cream cheese icing between the layers. Twenty gold candles are scattered on the surface of the cake, and after the caterer lights every one of them, he steps back so I can take the place of honor next to the cake.

The lights in the gallery grow dim, and I nibble at my lip while everyone surrounds me in a semi-circle. The guests look at me expectantly, and I cough, clearing my throat before speaking.

"I just want to thank everyone for coming out to celebrate not just my birthday, but the grand opening of the Gatt-Dieren Gallery. I'm touched that all of you came to spend this evening with us, and hope that we will have many more of these exhibits and parties to come in the future."

I fold my hands in front of me, not sure what to do next as the crowd murmurs amongst themselves, but the ice is broken when Matt yells from somewhere in the group, "Happy Birthday, Petra!"

As if on cue, the party launches into a cheery, if disorganized, rendition of the happy birthday song, and as the notes of the final words float through the air, I bend down and blow out my candles.

For a brilliant moment before the flames are extinguished, I can see the faces of my husband, friends, and family through them, shining like the bright jewels that they are. I blow on each candle one by one, filled with a contented sort of joy. This is everything I could have ever wanted for my birthday, and more.

This year, no wishes are even necessary.

CHAPTER 10

Manhattan, December 19, 2021
Petra

Alex grips the steering wheel even though we've stopped. His knuckles are white. "This is a mistake."

"You're overreacting," I tell him, starting to exit the car.

But he doesn't seem convinced and grabs my arm to stop me, "Petra, let's just go home. They're too young for this."

I shake him off, disbelieving. "You said we needed to go out with the kids more often, so I planned this outing for all four of us and *now* they're too young for it? Quit being weird!"

"We're going to Aspen in three days," he reminds me, causing a smile to spread up to my ears. The idea we're gonna spend our first Christmas together, the four of us, fills me with excitement. Geez, in just three days we'll finally be off to our winter residence but this time with our kids! It's crazy how fast time has passed, and the anticipation makes my heart flutter in my chest. "There will be plenty of suitable activities to do there with them."

"I'm sure they are gonna enjoy being in a pool," I insist, refocusing on the present issue. "And today it's perfect since the instructor was available for a private class."

I can see the tension in his jaw as he puts the car in park and takes a huge breath before blowing it out slowly. "We could have hired the teacher and done it in our own pool, you know."

"They told me their pool is suitable for infants, but they couldn't guarantee ours is," I tell him, making this up. Truthfully, I really just wanted to get out of the house and go somewhere new to spend some family time. "Jasper already loves water and Jasmine seems pretty okay with it, so I'm sure they're gonna be fine."

"Alright," he mutters. "But I still don't like it."

I give him another annoyed glance. Hopping out of the car and moving to the back door, I open it with a dramatic flourish that causes Jasmine to laugh, her lips drawn up in a grin that puts her gums on display.

"You ready for a special afternoon, princess?" I ask her, unhinging her car seat to carry her inside while Alex does the same for Jasper on the other side.

"We're going to need a new car sooner or later," he tells me casually as we head into the building.

I huff at his observation, my head shaking. "What are you talking about? This one is perfectly fine."

"As of right now it's okay, and it's got the bulletproof glass, so I'm not in too much of a hurry, but when they grow up, they'll need a bit more space in the back."

"You just want a new car," I say, sliding him a glance out of the corner of my eye. "Admit it." But he ignores me, using his hip to open the door to the glass and brick building, stepping out of the way so I can follow him inside.

The smell hits me immediately: chlorine and bleach, strong in the hot, humid air. It's a nostalgic smell that reminds me of the swimming classes of my own childhood.

Everything, from the floors to the walls, is tile, except for the wooden check-in desk with a bright-eyed receptionist sitting behind it.

"Take this," I tell Alex, handing him Jasmine's carrier and approaching the desk.

"Hi!" the receptionist says with a wide smile. "How can I help you?"

"We're here for the two pm Tadpoles swim class, two babies and two adults." I lower my voice, just in case anyone recognizes my name. "I made the booking under the name Petra Van Gatt."

"Wonderful," the receptionist says, her nails clicking rhythmically on the keyboard in front of her. "I've got you all checked in. You can take your little angels to the back wading pool. Here is your key card for your private family changing room. Enjoy!" She slides a key card across the counter to me and I pocket it.

"Thank you," I tell her, heading back to Alex.

He's taken a seat in one of the chairs dotting the lobby, having set both carriers down. The twins are wide-eyed and very awake, but quiet for the moment, taking in the blue and teal surroundings. Alex had brought in their diaper bag as well, brimming with white, fluffy towels. We are prepared, if not overly prepared, but Alex's face still seems tense.

"You ready to go get changed?" I ask him, my hands on my hips.

"I'm assuming I don't have any choice," he mumbles grumpily, rising from his seat and grabbing Jasper's carrier.

I know Alex has a valid point in thinking that a swimming class for infants is kind of crazy, but Lily had suggested I do some research into it and that she thought it would be a great experience.

After doing some reading, I had gotten more and more excited about the idea. The benefits of water time with young babies are huge, especially those like Jasmine, who are weaker than others her age.

The classes are less actual "swimming" and more spending time moving their bodies against the gentle resistance of the water to build strength in an easy, relaxing way. Floating is also good for the little ones, allowing them to relax their muscles while also building trust between parent and child. There is a reason why water exercise is used in physical rehabilitation after all!

"Will you just relax?" I ask him, keeping my voice low so no one else can eavesdrop. "It's not like we're training them for the Olympics or anything. It's just a children's swim class."

Alex's shoulders slump in resignation. "I know. I just don't enjoy taking unnecessary risks with them after all we've been through."

My annoyance with his resistance wanes. I still think this will be a wonderful experience for us, but I can sort of understand where he is coming from. "We want them to thrive, though, not just survive. For that, we need to take minor risks here and there. Plus, we'll be holding them the whole time."

"You're damn right we will," he insists, causing me to laugh.

I stop and kiss him on the cheek quickly before we head into the changing room. "You're very dramatic."

It would have been easier for us all to wear our suits to the swim class, but with it being nearly freezing outside, I had decided we would just change when we arrived. The whole facility is in one of the nicest parts of the city, and besides the specialty children's swim experiences, they also offer water aerobics classes, authentic Swedish saunas, and hot mineral soaks, so it's no surprise that their private family changing rooms are comfortable and borderline luxurious.

I tap the key card to the lock and the light above it turns green, allowing us inside. The floors are still tile but there are absorbent mats underneath the changing tables and in the shower to prevent slipping, along with our own lockers, a long wooden bench, and a mini fridge filled with cold bottled water.

Alex and I change first, him into simple black trunks and me into a red sporty one piece I had purchased for the occasion. I have drawers full of fashionable bikinis in pale shades that compliment my skin tone, but I have this vision in my head of one twin yanking down my top or undoing a tie when I'm not paying attention, so for once in my adult life I purchased a proper athletic bathing suit.

Alex raises his eyebrows when he sees me in it, and I shoot him a glare. "Shut up. It's a necessary evil and you know it."

"I didn't say a single thing," he replies, amused. "But if you ever want to pursue a career in lifeguarding, just let me know."

I fling a towel at him, and he laughs. As annoying as it is for him to poke fun at me, at least he is lightening up about the class.

We tag-team changing the twins, both in equally simple suits since the website for the class had said frilly or extravagant suits would get in the way. At least I was able to get them matching suits, both sporting a dark blue ensemble emblazoned with little orange goldfish. With their chubby legs and round bellies sticking out, the twins must be the cutest things on the planet.

When we're all changed, we head out the second frosted door in the back of the changing room and emerge into the wading pool area. I'm glad that it doesn't look as clinical and utilitarian as the pools of my childhood memories. Instead, the sides and edges of the large pool slope naturally down, including a gentle ramp for us to enter the water. It is noticeably hotter here, and I can feel the sweat beading on my forehead almost immediately. The overhead lights are bright LEDs, but the scenes of the forest painted on the walls nullify the harshness.

The instructor is already in the pool, a young woman with jet black hair tightly pulled into a ponytail and a blue bathing suit. The water reached her waist, and I'm glad we won't be going any deeper this time around. She beckons us into the water, her brilliantly white teeth gleaming in her smile.

"Welcome in, guys! My name is Alana, and I'll be showing you the ropes today. Since you've purchased the private class, it will be just us as I'm sure you already know."

I smile back, holding Jasmine tightly to me as I descend the ramp into the water. "Hi, Alana. I'm Petra, this little chunk is Jasmine, and that's my husband Alex with our bigger one, Jasper."

"Love the names," she says. "Is this your first time in a pool with them?"

I nod. "They were born in the summer, but they were preemies and swimming was just not in the cards."

Alex comes in after me, and Jasper, our water lover, seems to sense what's going on, and becomes increasingly excited about the prospect of an extra-large bath. His breathing is fast and loud, and he kicks his legs in anticipation.

The water is so warm that there is no hesitation as it brushes my calves and eventually my waist. Jasmine squeals as it laps at her feet, but I hold her out of the water mostly, letting her get used to the idea.

Alex, on the other hand, seems to be fighting a losing battle. Once the water touches Jasper's foot, he becomes obsessed, wiggling in his father's arms like a frantic fish. Alana raises an eyebrow and chuckles at the two of them.

"I guess it's time to get started, then," she declares happily.

She leads us through the first exercise of lowering the babies slowly in the warm water, letting them both adjust to being submerged instead of it being a shock. Jasper laughs loud enough to echo off the tile walls, but Jasmine is more reserved, watching me with a touch of apprehension in her blue eyes, as if to say, "I'm trusting you here, but I'm still not sure," but once she's up to her belly, she lets out a few inquisitive noises, splashing at the water with her hands.

I can sort of see why she'd be iffy about the situation. In the bath, they were always sitting on solid ground, but here, the only security they have is Alex and I's grip. Alana has us hold them in place until Jasmine is comfortable and Jasper has settled down before we could move on to some movements.

First, we spin in a circle slowly, holding the babies around the middle. They both kick and splash, the instinctual swimming movements that all babies have coming out. Alex is as tense as I've ever seen him, but Jasper's joy is infectious, and I can see the smile pulling at his mouth after a few minutes.

"Let them get a feel for the freedom of the water," Alana instructs. "Don't hold them with a tight grip, hold them loosely but securely so they have a range of movement."

We stop and start a few times, moving in circles and straight lines, letting the twin's reactions set the pace. Jasmine's tiny face is scrunched in concentration as she paddles her legs through the water. She seems to really think she's propelling herself, even though I'm the one moving her, and her stoic insistence on working hard is positively adorable. Jasper's "swimming" is more chaotic, his stronger legs kicking up enough water to soak Alex's hair. He sputters but ultimately laughs along with his son, bobbing him up and down in the water to both of their delights.

"Now, for the biggest part of our lesson today: floating. Hold your baby in front of you and slowly rotate them to their back and place your hands under their backs, not gripping, just supporting. Once they realize they are floating nearly on their own, they will become calm."

This is the part I know Alex has been the most concerned about, but he follows the instructor's directions. With Jasper's enthusiasm, Alex is having a harder time than me, but once he has him on his back the flailing subsides and Jasper seems almost serene, babbling quietly at the ceiling with his dad's hands supporting him as he floats.

Jasmine doesn't give me any sass, thankfully, and is easily moved into the floating position. Her tiny body is stiff with tension at first, but when she realizes she is safe and weightless, she relaxes into my supporting hands, a peaceful smile suffusing her face.

"Ma ma ma," she whispers, eyes fluttering.

"I think she's dozing off," I tell Alana in a quiet hiss.

"That means she trusts you and the water fully. She's completely at peace."

Alex looks over at us. His expression is soft and loving. I smile back at him, and we both enjoy the quiet moment with our twins, all four of us completely at ease.

"I told you so," I murmur to Alex, who sighs, looking at the ceiling briefly with a long-suffering look.

"I guess you did, didn't you?"

* * *

Once the class is over, we go back inside our changing room, the kids already half-sleeping in our arms, wrapped in dry towels.

"It was such a great class, wasn't it?" I ask Alex in a whisper so as not to wake them up.

"Much better than I thought," he admits before he starts rinsing Jasper off at the showers. I do the same with my little princess, who opens her eyes wide once she feels the warm water coating her skin. My heart is full, filled with gratitude to have spent such a great time in the water with my two little mermaids. After the twins are fully clothed, Alex heads to the shower while I take a moment to check if I received the photos Alana sent me. She was kind enough to take a few pictures of us at the end of the class and I couldn't wait to go and check them out. I plug in my phone and see a few unread messages. I find Alana's and the beautiful photos we took during the class, but I also find another SMS. This one though is from a Dutch number I don't recognize. Curiosity taking the better of me, I click on it and start reading: *"Thank you so much to have invited me to Aspen for Christmas. I can't wait to see the four of you very soon. We're gonna have such a great time together. Best wishes, Margaret."*

WHAT! I nearly drop my phone in shock. What did I just read? It's impossible! Not her! Not Margaret! Why is she even thanking me to have invited her? I never did that!

Unless…

My attention goes to the person standing tall inside the shower and my nerves start boiling under my skin, thinking about the probability that it was Alex who invited her on our behalf. *"Petra and I would be delighted to have you with us,"* I picture him saying to his mom.

I swallow the lump in my throat, filled with anger and sadness. I can't believe she's joining us for our first solo family trip in just a few days. What a nightmare… I look at the screen of my phone again, focusing in on the text message, making sure I read it properly. Damn, it really was Margaret.

"Are you okay?"

My eyes drift to where the voice is coming from and I find Alex standing tall out of the shower, a white towel wrapped around his hips, confusion laced all over his face.

After taking a few deep breaths, I finally say, "We need to talk."

TO BE CONTINUED…